How the Hell Do We Get Home From Here?

How the Hell Do We Get Home From Here?

The Awakening

James Willman

Copyright © 2011 by James Willman.

Library of Congress Control Number: 2011919199
ISBN: Hardcover   978-1-4653-8724-0
                Softcover   978-1-4653-8723-3
                Ebook   978-1-4653-8725-7

All rights reserved. No part of this book may be reproduced or transmitted in any form or by any means, electronic or mechanical, including photocopying, recording, or by any information storage and retrieval system, without permission in writing from the copyright owner.

This is a work of fiction. Names, characters, places and incidents either are the product of the author's imagination or are used fictitiously, and any resemblance to any actual persons, living or dead, events, or locales is entirely coincidental.

This book was printed in the United States of America.

To order additional copies of this book, contact:
Xlibris Corporation
1-888-795-4274
www.Xlibris.com
Orders@Xlibris.com
105040

*A special thanks to my beautiful
wife, Mom, Grandma and dad.
Thanks for believing in what I can do.*

Chapter 1

Rweee! An alarm goes off and echoes in to a dream.
"I will kill you!" A muscular man stabs a spear down past Vander's eyes. At the last minute his metallic hand hits the blade. Sparks fly as it grinds across his hand and rocks whip past him falling to the ground.
Rweee!

Light hits the figure and he can see him clearly. Joe? The name rings fast in his head, the pencil line beard framing his face a dead giveaway. Questions flood the mind: how did he get taller, where did he get a leather outfit, and what's with the hat that has no bill?

Rweee!

Joe gets to his feet as He starts to raise his spear. Vander reaches down and grabs Joe's hand closest to him, rolls his shoulder into his arm, Joe loses his balance then Vander punches him square in the teeth.

Rweee!

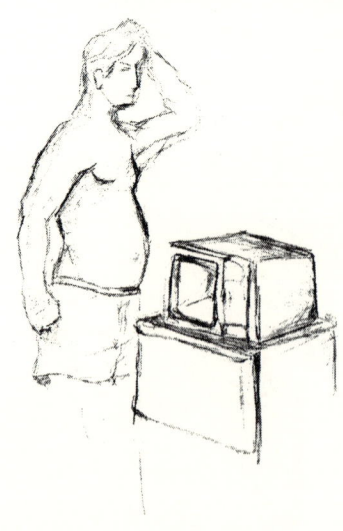

White out. It is black in the dorm room. The alarm sounds off a few more times before he hits the right button. Vander sits up in a sweat, a six foot guy with a gut that he calls a love tank, he starts scratching his head. He grimaces at what he considers a waste of human flesh sleeping in his room. "*Dorm life,*" He thinks to himself hoping he'll move out soon so he can get a better roommate.

"Ugh, Saturday morning work." He lets out a big yawn and stumbles to the bathroom to do his morning ritual. Holding the sides of the sink, he can't shake the thought of Joe shoving a spear into his face. "This one I have to tell Nick about."

He cleans up and puts on work clothes for his bagel shop job and heads out of the room, slamming the door behind him, hoping to wake up the roommate. He walks a little ways, then goes downstairs and heads to the back of the complex. Room 114, the door says. Vander pounds on the door and waits a few minutes for the door to open. Nick, a skinny, six-foot-one guy in nothing but boxers, opens the door while rubbing his eyes. "You have to be kidding." He opens the door wider and lets Vander in. Vander sits down. Nick puts on a similar outfit—beige pants and a black shirt with goofy-looking bagel logos covering the front.

"I just had the weirdest dream ever. Joe was trying to kill me with a spear. He was loaded up on steroids and covered in buckles and leather straps."

"Joe, my roommate? You know what they say. The more buckles the cooler the character. Look at Jackson."

"Yeah, but that wasn't it. I had a metal hand and could grab the blade and not get hurt."

They leave the room. Nick lights up a clove cigarette. On the side of the complex is a fence, and jumping it cuts the walk to work almost in half. They walk along a canal wall to a bridge, finally crossing the water.

"What do you think about that dream?"

"Dude, you're losing it. Joe is cocky but not enough to 'roid out and come after you. Maybe finals got to you."

A few minutes later, they arrive at work, Bagels and Bagels. Nick takes the front where people order, and Vander slaps the food together. Four hours go by, and the breakfast rush slows down. The guys start to joke around with each other by this time. The door opens up; and Jenifer, the cutest girl in school, shows up, carrying a stack of flyers.

How the Hell Do We Get Home From Here?

Nick's jaw drops. "Well helloooo." She comes hopping to the counter with a giant smile.

"So you wanna come out to this party and hang out with me and my friends? I have a private booth right next to the stage." She smiles and thrust her hand out to Nick, holding a flyer. Nick reaches out, grabs her thumb, and caresses her hand until he takes the flyer. She giggles and bites her thumb. "I'll take that as a yes. I can't wait to see you there. Save a seat for me on your lap." She bounces out, catching up with her friends.

Nick looks over at Vander and the two other guys staring at him and the whole situation. He finally breathes out. "Holy shit, dude." The guys hoot and holler at him.

"Oh, you sly dog, you!"

"You got the moves!"

Vander smirks at him and walks over. "I'm just glad that we didn't have to pick you up off the floor."

Nick laughs. "Oh shit, man, I can't believe I finally did something. I've only been helping her out with her work for a week!"

Joe walks in. He is "the closer." The name speaks for itself, but yes, he and a few others close down the store today. "Hey, guys!" he says, picking up his apron and putting it around his waist.

"Man, you just missed Nick's smooth moves on Jenifer," the cashier says.

"It's about goddamn time. Your three-week time limit was almost up. I would have had to step in and bang her." Joe says with a grin, leaning back and stroking his pencil-thin beard. Then he laughs as Nick's face changes. "Just joking, buddy. I could tell that you wanted her. You could never get out from under the desk when she came over."

"Not my fault. She wears low-cut shirts when she comes over, and the last time she did, we made out when you left."

The boys start up again, louder this time. The door opens. Nick calms them down and goes to take an order. Joe takes his place right next to Vander on the line, getting ready to help with the lunch rush.

"Oh man, at this rate, I may have to sleep on your couch a couple of nights during the week," Joe says. "The great part about that is we can start pushing that big nose out of your room!"

"Yeah, that would be nice. Then we'll move Chris in and party like the old days BBN."

"What's BBN?"

"Before Big Nose!"

Nick brings the ticket and the flyer over and puts both in the order hanger. "So are we going or not?"

"Going? Like I'm going to hold out on an abandoned warehouse party."

Joe butts in, "But the party is for people of legal age, and last time I checked, we're all nineteen."

Vander replies coyly, "Oh yes, they are really going to stop us at the door and not let us spend our money in there. Just like all the other parties that we have crashed."

Nick laughs. "It's a hard knock life." They laugh and continue to work.

Vander goes on break when Nick comes back. Joe starts cleaning things, lifting out bins, and taking extra food back to the cooler. He looks over at Vander. "I have a crazy thought. What would you do if you were Jesus? You know, the savior."

Vander replies jokingly, "I'd be pissed that I'm already dead."

Joe laughs a little and continues, "No, if you had the powers of, like, God and could heal everything or destroy anything."

"Oh well, then . . . I might show my face every so often and let people know why they should worship me. I really like the idea of forcing a utopia on the masses."

"Me, I would be around all the time. I'd kill every bastard that got in my way. Plus, I would make a holy army to help me run everything."

"Wow, you have all this planned out. You spent all night thinking about it."

"No, no, just over a six-pack. And as the bottles went by, I go meaner and meaner as God."

"True. I would hate to have damn dirty hippies running around. Then there would be bagel shops on every corner, and monkeys like us would have to work our butts off to feed the masses!"

"Nooooo!" Joe falls to his knees. Vander bursts out laughing.

The whole line stops and stares. Vander helps him up. "Its only bagel hell. The hippies will still be well fed!" Some of the customers scoff but don't leave the line.

"But yeah, I would get rid of all the goddamn deserts. Nobody needs those things, and I'm tired of dying in those levels in video games. You always get sucked down by something, and it's never something that you would love to have sucking you. And I especially hate when they make you find a fucking underground cave—in the *desert*!"

Nick slides over, sliding in a ticket this time. "So you going to come to this party? We need the group together to get into this, A-Team party-crasher style!"

"Well, Albert, Stoner and Stinky are always willing to join us in our ventures. With that size group, they wouldn't mind letting us in." Joe laughs, slapping cream cheese on a bagel.

They continue to work, cleaning up their stations to help Joe get a head start on the closing of the store. But it's Monday, and Vander and Nick have class today at five. The class hates that they don't have time to go home and shower, but the free food they bring in calms them down. Their class is math. At this school, everyone starts in this class. It's like math for dumb jocks that need a helper course to get in a special ed class. This class made Nick and Vander want to pass out for the next three hours to catch up on sleep. But then, Vander stops and begins to stare at Sandra and Sasha coming in the room and giggling. They sit next to our boys.

Nick kicks Vander. "Dude, you're going to blow it again if you don't pull it together!"

Sandra looks over at Vander. "You're in my Basic Drawing 2 class. How come? Aren't you just a freshman?"

Vander shakes his head a little and rubs the back of his neck. "Yeah, I worked really hard over the last summer and brought them a stellar portfolio. So they skipped me ahead and put me with the tough teacher, just to make sure I'm legit."

Sandra looked at him. "I can't believe I have to carry this sketchbook everywhere or everyone will get extra work. I don't even have a bag that will fit it."

"Hey, let me take a look."

Sandra smiles a toothy, wide-open smile. "Really." She pulls it off her desk and hands it over.

Vander opens the black book and starts running through the pages. Each page had bad art—no shading, all profiles or faces of characters with one heavy line. He didn't know what to say, but wanting to make her his, he smiled and nodded. "Oh, I like this one."

She asks for his; he hands it over. On the first page, her reply is, "Oh, damn, this is good! Way better than mine!"

Vander looks for an In. "No, I like your stuff. Especially this one, part demon, part angel."

"That is Gal-en-daruis! She is my greatest story. She is a demon that fell from heaven and is looking for a lover. Anytime she is not happy with the man, she turns him into a mindless slave."

Vander laughs. "So she marries them."

Sandra giggles back. "No, not exactly. She wires them into a super computer that she can talk to, and they have to do her bidding."

The teacher stands up. "All right, class, time to get started. Thank you, Vander and Nick, for the food, but now we need to get going."

Vander slips Sandra a flyer. She grabs it and looks it over. She whispers, "I'm already going, so is Sasha. I hope I'll meet you there. I'm going to be upstairs. I helped set up. So I arranged a special room."

Vander sits up. "I'll be looking for ya!"

The teacher starts writing some math problems on the board. "Okay, let's continue and try to learn fast so that we can get done early. I'm trying to beat my last time, where we got out three weeks early."

The class continues, and it's so simple that Nick is moving along nicely, answering anything the teacher asks. Nick was in Pre-Calculus before he came here, but since he is a science major, they had to start him here to "*make sure he doesn't miss out on anything.*" When class ends, Vander and Nick are left to clean up the food, allowing everyone to leave before them. They go back to their dorms and get ready to be the life of the party.

A few calls are made, and everyone meets up at Vander's dorm, A-4. They could meet elsewhere, but Vander has all the systems and *two* TVs! Last one to arrive is Joe, being that he just finished work and wanted to relax.

"Hey, bitches! Who's ready for an ass kickin'!" He laughs as he picks up a controller. "Going to rock your world like I would if I was God!"

"Wow, you must have thought about that all day!" Vander laughs, throwing a drawing eraser. The room was full. Stoner, Scoobs (because he is always eating), and Eric are all over 265 pounds, plus Pepto, Steve-Dave, Fred, Frank, and Gavin—you know, the guys. "Man, I wish the girls met here too. This seems to be quite the sausage fest."

"Shut it, or we're not going to show up until we have to leave." Stone laughed. "Now I'm going to take you down like the clown that you are."

"You can't spank a god!" Joe laughs. "Bow down before me!"

The boys get rowdy after each playing an hour of fighting games. Then they load up in three cars and head to the party. It's not far from the dorms. The old hotels next to the warehouse district were more convenient for the school to buy. By that we mean they were cheep.

The group pulls up and pours out of the cars. The surrounding area has run-down, abandoned buildings in all levels of disarray. Only a few have lights on in them and chain-link fences to keep people out. As they make it to the door, a bouncer meets them at the front door. A big black guy stands at the door. Most of the guys in the party are around six foot tall and large.

"Hey, Larges!" Vander yells.

The bouncer turns to him. "Hey, guys, how's it going!" They pound fists. "What's up, you guys heading out tonight?"

Vander laughs and puts up his hand. "Eh, you know, coach, we're not travelin' far."

"Come on, man, you need to try somewhere else. I know you're underage, and I shouldn't let you in."

Nick says, "Oh come now, you know we tip good and treat the ladies nice, just like the bar wants us too. So you can mark the *X* on our hands, and we have the acetone to take it off."

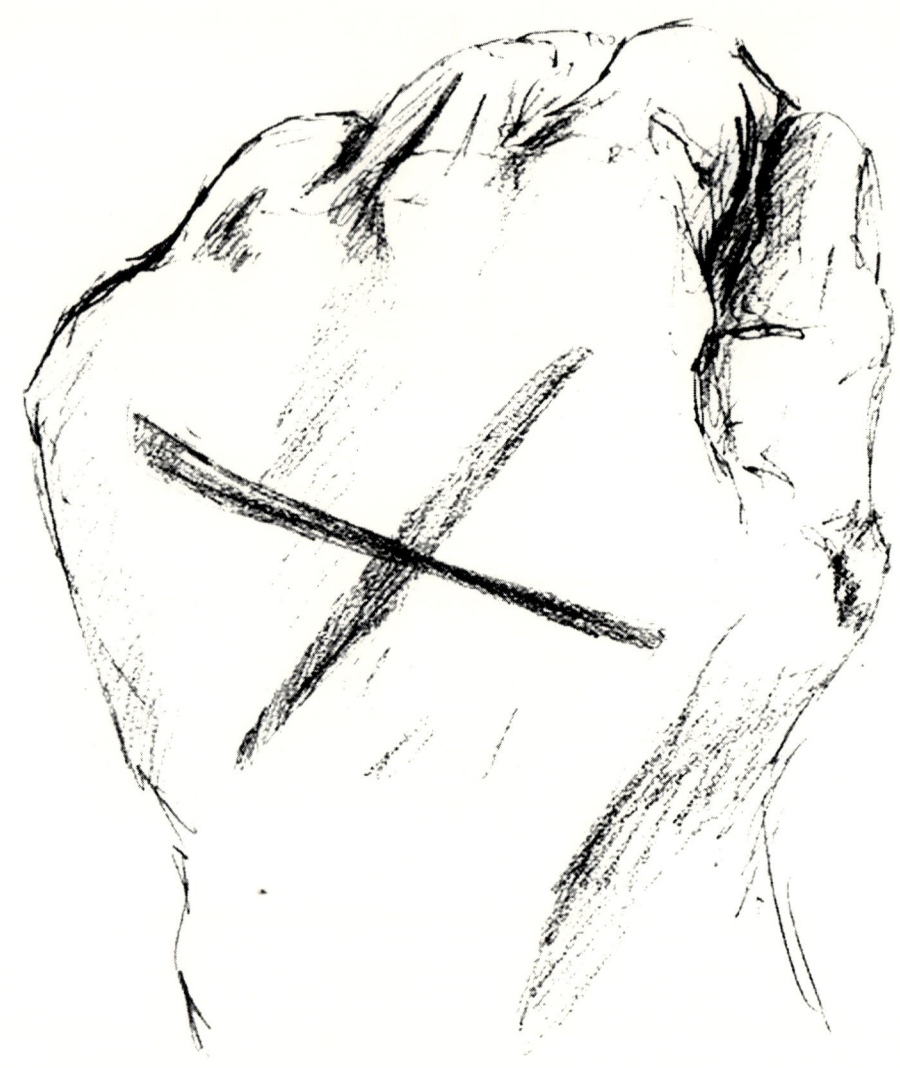

"You know I have to say something before letting you in." Larges laughs and shakes Joe's hand. "Thanks, but be careful. One of these days, your tips is going to pay off my student loans and you'll have to bribe someone else, then I'll be a real teacher and only have to work with kids during the day."

"Anything to help." Joe laughs, patting him on the shoulder. "Don't worry, coach. We'll have you out of the bouncing business in no time."

"Hey, how about not getting into any more fights? Last time, I killed a man because of you!"

"Deal." Joe gives two thumbs up as they walk in.

"I mean it!"

On the inside of the building, there is scaffolding running all along the roof of the place with stage lights hanging, lighting the place up in tons of colors. The light sets up a sort of barrier; the people tend to stay in a three-foot square around the table. There is a main dance floor right in front of the DJ's stand, where the first DJ is already spinning records. A platform is elevated four feet up with a makeshift banister running along the edge so that people won't fall over. From the top looking down, it looks like a blocky V shape; old musty couches line the parameter. When they walk in, there is a bar serving drinks and a large crowd around it. When customers leave, they carry pitchers of drinks with them to their groups.

Scoobs and Stoner got to the front of the group. Wide-eyed Stoner says, "Guys, two groups up, girls that need our attention!"

"I get the fat one!" Scoobs turns and starts leading the way.

Pepto laughs and looks at Vander and Nick. "You ever get the feeling that Scoobs is the fat chick of our group? I'm so glad he's here though, makes me look like prince charming."

The guys laugh. They choose to go to the orange section, where the girls are. They start singling out which one they want to be with and start circling up around a table that has a couple of pitchers of alcohol and juices. Nick starts mixing drinks and handing them out to anyone who asks. The music gets louder, and people start grinding on each other. Some are even dirty dancing; it's shameless, but what else are you supposed to do at a party like this?

Nick looks up at the main stage. It's an old pal, Deej—a lanky guy wearing big dark glasses, a black cut shirt, and big ol' baggy jeans. Nick tugs on Vander's arm and points. Vander notices, then they both wave, and Deej waves them to come up. They agree mainly because some of the hotter girls are already up there and the better drinks are *for free*! A bunch of songs go by, and the temporary club/warehouse fills with fun goers ready to shut the place down. Deej points to Nick that they are out of orange juice. Nick grabs the pitcher and starts making his way over to the bar. He only has to wait a few minutes before he gets his drink. Even though he doesn't have to pay, he still leaves a big tip. The guys are known for this, and this is why they get service first before anyone else. Life is good. Nick starts heading back, holding the juice to his chest. The music skips, making Nick look up. *That never happens*, he thinks to himself.

Vander and Deej aren't there. A scream breaks out but is cut short as the screamer and a group around her fall to the ground. A person walks up to the group and falls to the ground; the people behind her fall to the ground. He backs up and turns to the front; people are already falling to the ground that way too. He heads to the side of the building to the bathroom. He thinks, *There has to be a window there*. He starts pushing people out of the way. He grabs for the door and opens it. A man falls on top of him. He shoves him to the side as the body falls to the ground. Time slows down. He feels like he has been hit by a pro boxer; the lines of the world blur. He can't move; people dancing all around hit the floor. He slides down with his back against the wall, sits with his knees against his chest, and finally lowers his head. All goes black.

Chapter 2

Vander wakes up dizzy, shakes his head, and sits up. His head pounds. He pulls up his legs and rests his arms on them. *How did I get in the grass?* he thinks. *I was at a party, I fell asleep somehow, but where am I now?* To his left, he sees a tree line, a road, and a sign on top of the nearby hill. He seems to be sitting in a wheat field but the plants are still young. He looks to his right, and there is a strange creature.

"Aahhh!" Vander reacts, scooting away. The creature doesn't stir. The creature has drool coming out of his mouth. Vander looks around and finds a stick nearby. He pokes the creature with it.

"Vander, cut that out, you fat bastard!" the creature says as he stands up. As he stretches, he wipes the drool off of his chin.

"What are you looking at?" asks Nick. As he finishes wiping his mouth, he stands up, scratching his butt.

Vander is looking at a four-eleven alien-looking creature. He has a large oval head; arms that hang down to its knees on his short, stumpy legs; and large feet to top it off.

"You! Where am I? Who are you, and how do you know me?" Vander scrambles back a few feet and stands.

"Dude?" Nick is surprised by Vander's reaction. "It's me, Nick . . . your best friend! I don't think I even know any more than you." He looks around, surveying the surroundings.

"You can't be Nick! Nick is tall and skinny."

"What are you talking about? I'm still me!" Nick looks down and notices that he is looking straight into Vander's eyes, but Vander is still only sitting up. "Whahappened to me?" He holds his hands out in front of him and looks over his body.

"I don't know. Is it really you?" Vander moves over to poke him.

"*Yes*, it's really me. I see you're still your stupid self . . . Hey, wait a minute, why am I practically naked and you're dressed all different? Ahh, what the shit!"

"I admit, these clothes are cool, but hey, don't blame this on me!" Vander gets in his face, thumb to his chest.

"Well, it's most likely your fault!" Nick climbs on Vander's chest and pulls on his shirt while staring him in the eyes.

* * *

"Let's try and get some answers. There's a road, and trees. This is too weird. It's like starting a video game or something." Music starts to play, and they make heroic stances.

How the Hell Do We Get Home From Here?

"Yeah, where is the white rabbit?" Vander asks.
"How about a brown one?" replies Nick.

Vander looks around. There's a rabbit-type animal, big and brown. The colors are spottier than usual; its hair color goes lighter from back to front. The legs are long for a rabbit, and there is a ball on its long doglike tail.

"Wow, look at it come right up to us. He's brave or used to humans."

Vander says, "Sure is weird looking."

Vander walks over to it. He kneels down and starts petting it; it seems docile. The rabbit-looking thing growls and snaps at him. Vander yelps, "Shit!" Vander kicks; it falters a little. Nick jumps in and punches it. It falls back, shakes its head and sneers, then runs off. Vander picks up a rock and chucks it. It knocks it in the head. It stops, turns to look at them, and falls dead.

Bewildered, Vander says, "That is the weirdest thing I ever saw. Except for you."

Nick replies, "You know that I'm really going to kick your ass. What are we going to do now?"

"I don't know, but are you hungry?"

"Yeah, but are you sure we can eat something that looks like it ate uranium?"

"We've got nothing else."

They gather materials for a fire. Standing in front of the wood and rocks, they look at each other. Nick scrunches his face. "You don't have matches in there, do you?" Vander shakes his head. Nick bends down, grabs two dry pieces of wood, then begins to rub them together. Nick closes his eyes and says, "Come on, fire!" A spark ignites the tip of the wood. He quickly sets it in the pile at the bottom. The rest slowly kindle. "I guess don't look a gift horse in the mouth." They make it rotisserie style, cooking it till it looks almost black.

With a mouth half full of food, Nick says, "You know, I can't tell where the hell we are. The vegetation and animals are giving me no clues. This is all stuff I can almost say I've never seen."

"We did see a road earlier. At least there is civilization around."

"We're going to have to follow it. It's got to lead somewhere. Then we can get some answers."

They finish eating, leaving a good portion for the morning. After a few hours of talking, they lie down and go to sleep.

* * *

Tink tink tink . . . tink phssssst. The sound of hydraulic pistons letting out air. Vander wakes up and sees a man on top of him. His face has a scar in a U shape from his lips through his eyes and two more leading from the corners of his lips to his ears.

The man joyfully greets him, "Hiya!"

In shock, Vander again jumps from his sleep and screams, "Ahh! Why does that happen so much here?"

The man does not move and continues to stare. Vander realizes he's not aggressive.

"Uh . . . hi, how did you find us here?"

The man replies back, "Quick with questions."

Vander reaches over and shakes Nick by the shoulder.

"Ahhh!" He reacts the same way, jumping back.

The man points at Vander. "He just said that. Is that what you say when you first meet people where you're from?"

Nick cocks his head and squints his eyes. "No." He moves in for a closer look at the man's legs. "Your legs are metal and inverted."

The man stands up and cocks his head to the side mockingly. "You act like you've never seen this before."

Vander stands up and looks him in the eyes. "Um . . . we haven't."

The man, with a smug look, answers, "You've got to be joking." He pauses to make sure it's not a joke. "I'm one of Oglathorpe's mail carrier. We've all been fused with magitech."

Nick continues inspecting the legs, getting closer and touching them. The inverted legs are designed like a cat's hind legs; they are sleek but come to a point. They lead up to where his hips should be; instead, there's a hemisphere with flesh overlapping the edges. The ball sits on top of a ring of gadgets that connect to the legs. He carries a backpack, a blanket, plus a pouch at his side. His body is heavily scarred where it connects to his tech. You can see the line of wires up his spine that blink sporadically when he moves. From all the running, mail carriers are muscular and usually have long hair. "We don't get to stay in one place very long and are timed between drops, so there is no time for luxury. I am one of Joe's mechanical slaves. My name is Akhem the runner."

The name rings a bell in Vander's mind. "Who is Joe?"

Nick is now crawling all over the man's legs. Even Akhem is watching him.

Akhem is still moving in weird ways to accommodate Nick. "You must be from the bad lands. No? How about the calm? Those are the only places he really doesn't go. He's a religious leader that is bent on world domination. Everyone knows, but no one dares defy him."

Nick is bent over one of the legs and looks up at him. "Why?" Akhem reaches down and pulls him up by his pants. Nick holds onto the band, trying to prevent a megawedgie.

Akhem breathes out hard in disgust. "Because they usually die."

Vander crosses his arms. "I'm surprised you found us."

Nick, still struggling to hold himself up, says, "I'm surprised he speaks English, so whoa!" He falls forward and hits the ground with his head and folds his arms under him like he is listening to a good story.

Still grinning at what had happened, Akhem questions, "Okay, what's English?"

Vander, grinning still, says, "You just spoke it."

"That's what they call it now?" Akhem's hand flies up from a relief of pressure. Nick falls out of his pants and scrambles to a nearby bush.

Vander and Akhem laugh. Vander replies, "Yeah. Well, where we're from."

"I was used to calling it Namako, and everyone speaks it all over this world. Ever since Joe made this world, there have been barely any other languages. He believes in unity of the species."

Nick is waiting with his hand out of the bush, implying that he wants his shorts. "Tell us more about Joeism."

How the Hell Do We Get Home From Here?   37

Akhem, with a look of confusion, says, "Weird that you don't know anything about Joe. He used to be a Yaw Bus. They ruled for many years, and they proclaimed that magic is a limited source and that machines will have to be the next dominating force of our society. Joe took power and enforced this even more. He has even taken the liberty to try and gather as many magical things in this world. We used to celebrate our diversities in magic and being, but now we are just one big mess."

Vander sarcastically asks, "You agree with Joeism then, huh?"

Akhem misses the subtle change in his voice. "No. I miss the old days and hope the prophecy comes true about the ancients coming back and setting this all straight."

Nick comes out of the bush, pulling up his shorts. "How do they work? Do you need to be plugged in at night?"

Akhem smiles and narrows his eyes. "My legs are a fusion of magic and metal. Joe discovered how the two could be fused together. A bunch of men were subjected to horrible experiments that ultimately made us. Many died, and the rest were forced to serve as empire slaves. Like me, I get to go everywhere, but I have to carry heavy things. Hey, I smell Cho Grizzerd. Do you have any left?"

"What's that?" asks Vander.

"I see some of the bones over there." Akhem points to the pile near the smoldering fire. "It's very good and hard to find!"

They give him some of their leftovers. He eats most of it, including marrow and cartilage.

Akhem, with his mouth half full, asks, "Are you heading towards Gnachvilla?"

Nick looks at him sideways. "Is that the closest town?"

"Yes, it's just up this road." He points with the leg of the animal.

"Then let's go paint the town red!" Nick pulls out a can of red paint and brush, then points the brush in the air.

With a confused look, Vander asks, "How did you do that?"

Nick looks at the items and sets them down. "I don't know. I just thought of making a joke with these items and voilà, here they are."

Akhem, still chewing and standing behind him, says, "Ah, you know magic? You better keep that a secret, or someone may come after you. Magic is used a lot, but your species is hunted because their essence can be pulled out."

"Guess so. That's awesome." Nick pauses to think. "But what about that last part? You know, about getting hunted."

Akhem shrugs his shoulders. "Should've known, you Gias usually have some kind of magic in you."

Nick looks at himself in amazement. "So that's what I am?"

Akhem starts to shake his legs. "So let's get going."

They leave for the town. It takes a few hours till they hit the edge of town. Akhem fills them in on the wonders of the local land. The road is rather narrow but still has two sides for carriages coming and going, even though it was rare. When they reached town, all the buildings look as though they were balls with chunks taken out for doors and windows. Some of the better-looking ones have a cylinder that leads to a rounded slat shingle roof, closer to terra-cotta style. Most of the two-story buildings have porches and scaffolding that lead from building to building, like another town that sits on top of a town. Homes are on the bottom, and storefronts are in the air. In the middle of the town is a large glowing generator, a giant crystal that pulses with light. It looks to be the most modern thing in the town. Akhem explains to them that it was some more magitech.

As for townsfolk, most are working in fields just outside of town; local shops are run by skeleton crews until sundown. Magitech is all over: Doors and windows open by themselves. Lights, heaters, and huge machines are connected to the buildings. Some people are flying on long metallic boards; some are sleek and others rounded like a 1950s car but squashed. Many others are riding giant monsterlike beasts. Some of the beasts have a gaping hole in their backs where other animal people would guide them by putting their bodies into it, like a gooey cockpit. You still see most of their bodies, but the arms and feet are immersed. Men walk around with melee weapons and armor. Some are officials of the law, but to their surprise, they can't see guns on so many heavily armed people.

For the most part, things are like a fantasy town, and with the fantasy town comes the fantasy people. Most are humanoids, meaning they walk on two legs but are all animalistic in features. A wide variety of these animal people—pigs, horses, cows, and many others—have personalities that seem to match the animals. There are smaller more insect-like people that have exoskeletons. They look like marionette puppets with the way the lower jaw fit in their facial structure. With rounded features and squinted small eyes, these creatures have color variations; all of them are about five feet tall and similar in shape. One other species have large chins that look like bags filled with water and stretch marks. They are muscular and bulky; most of them are green in this land, but they are known for having many colors as well.

After passing a few houses in the town, Akhem raises his arm and points. "Okay, there is the bar. Over there is a magi tower. Watch for the thugs in this trading arena. No one will find your body if you happen to make them mad."

Vander kneels down to Nick. "Okay, number one, let's make this home base till we get to know more about this place, world, or wherever we are."

Nick rubs his hands together. "No, number one, let's head to the bar first. I need a shot of whiskey after all this."

Akhem starts to run off. "Good luck!" Nick and Vander turn to him and see him starting to trot through town.

Vander keeps up. "Hey, can't you stay till we get settled in or something?"

Akhem, still jogging, says, "I wish I could. We will be friends, and I come this way many times so I can be on the lookout."

Vander returns to Nick. "Looks like we're on our own again. I hope this doesn't become a habit."

Nick scratches his head. "Alright, number two, we need to live, so get what we need. Money, house, and food. A job will have to be a necessary task."

They continue to walk to the bar. The doors are traditional swing doors hanging on a rounded entrance. The two-story bar has stairs leading to something like a porch that wraps around the walls and has rounded doors. A chandelier hangs low and is covered with wires, each leading to a bulb at the end. Eight tables are spread throughout the floor, and behind the bartender is a wall of liquor. The majority of people inside are pig, cow, and horse people. They're playing cards and listening to the music from a jukebox. A little pig man only four feet tall is wiping glasses and staring down the customers. His hands have three fingers; the tips look as though they are hooves working on being fingers. The black tips fade into flesh.

Vander sits at the bar. Nick struggles to get up on the barstool, swinging his legs and taking different grips on the chair but still not making it. The pig man snorts and squints his eyes. "What?"

Vander leans in on his elbows. "Hey, what can a guy do in this town to make a living?"

The bartender keeps watching Nick still struggling to get up on the stool. He looks back at Vander and eyes him slightly, taken aback that anyone would ask at a bar. He looks back at Nick. "Want a Gaia's stool?"

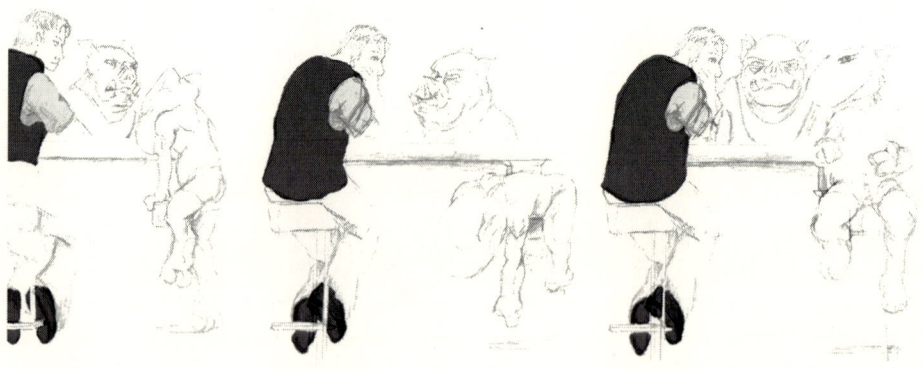

Nick looks over to another of his newly found kind; he is sitting on a stool that has a small staircase connected to it. With fire and determination in his eyes, he defiantly replies, "No!"

The bartender looks back at Vander. "I haven't seen your talent, but you can be a bouncer for me. I need an extra bouncer since I just fired my last one for showing up late too many times. So you're on tonight. Always need more bodies."

Vander looks at the crowd tonight; most are a foot shorter than him. "Okay, thanks. What about housing? I just brushed in and need somewhere to crash for now."

Nick finally gets to the top. He's breathing heavily, and he looks angry. Both hands on the bar and arms are straight. He takes a deep breath to calm himself.

The bartender watches the whole act and looks back at Vander. "If you're going to be the bouncer, you can live upstairs. Just *do not* touch the income. No freebies. I have only one room right now." As though the words came true, a loud, rustling noise is heard upstairs.

"Damn bitch! Now you're dead." A woman comes crashing over the railing, landing on a table and shattering it.

The bartender raises his brow and looks back at him. "Now I have two."

In amazement, Vander says, "Wow, we're pretty lucky. What about my friend here? Any jobs?"

The bartender looks over to Nick again. "You may want to try the tower. There's not many jobs for Gias on account of how they are."

Nick takes offense to the comment as though the bartender is insinuating he's homosexual. "Hey, I'm not that way!"

The bartender looks at him funny. "What way?"

"Gay," he replies as he crosses his arms.

He looks back in disgust. "What? The tower is a magic place for learning and using magic. Giasare rare creatures that do that shit."

Nick says, "Oohhhh. I used to know a club named the Tower. That's all." He rubs his head, hoping that he believed his bluff.

Vander sees a woman in a low-cut dress, raises one brow, and stares.

Nick asks, "What's your name?"

The bartender answers, "Mineo."

Nick puts out his hand. "Looks like we have a deal. We'll take both rooms, and I'll be upstairs."

Nick's eyes follow Vander's eyes. She is a beautiful human girl serving drinks to the locals. He plops down one elbow on the table. "Hello, I'm in love."

The girl gives a look of confusion and rubs the back of her neck. "Um, really?"

For the rest of the night, Vander chases the girl around, getting to know her and slowly winning her over. Nick goes up to pick which room he likes better. He picks the hooker's room first. The man is still inside, going through the drawers, picking up underwear, smelling it, then shoving it into his satchel. He looks over to Nick. "Get out of here."

Nick replies, "Well, this is my room now. So please leave."

The man stands up, snarling his lip. He puts the satchel over his shoulder as he approaches Nick.

"I'm not afraid of you!"

The man raises his brow higher. "You will before you die."

"You're the fifth human I've seen in this city. What's your story?"

The man narrows his eyes. "This must be a trick. You're here to take me in, *aren't you*! I'm not *going* to see Joe. You're going to *die*!" He rushes in to grab him. Nick falls back, yelling, "Vander!"

Vander stops talking and heads up the stairs. Halfway up, a loud bang comes from the room. Vander picks up his pace and sees the door open, his best friend on the floor and a guy ready to hit him. Vander flies into the air, landing his elbow on the man's head, forcing him onto the wall. Vander reaches back with his fist. Nick yells, "Hit him hard!" A mist surrounds his fist, and three times as fast as he's ever hit someone, his fist collides with the man's face. The man's eyes roll back. He slumps over, pushing Vander onto Nick; they both push him off. He rolls over like a bag of potatoes. The bouncer that is on duty comes in and helps drag him out of the bar, tossing him in the dirt. The bouncer starts going through the man's pockets, taking any money he had. "That's the toll for making me work!"

Nick pulls Vander aside. "That was odd. He thought I was here to take him to Joe."

Vander looks down at him. "What was weird is, when we were taking him down the stairs, he was getting lighter every step."

Nick moves around him. "Where did he go?" The body has disappeared, leaving behind just an imprint in the dirt, no traces of how he left. Nick shakes his head. "I need to think. I'm going to bed. I'll talk more in the morning." He heads to his room.

The bouncer comes over and gives Vander a sack with money. "Here's your half." He tightens his money bag to his belt. "So you and I will be working together. I'm Benny. That should be it for tonight. We actually only get one or two per night."

"Hey, thanks. I got your back if you have mine." Vander goes back inside the bar, watching the waitress start to close up the bar. He thinks about what he and his friends would be saying. "Lusty busty," Nick might say. Her name is Emily. She is five feet five; she's a fourteen, Vander guesses, or a sixteen. Most of the weight is in her hips. He feels embarrassed about drooling over her in their first meeting, so he buys her a drink—well, adds it to his tab. He turns on his charm; and as things slow, he helps clear tables and take bills, making sure she got her tips. Finally, they speak in length. The conversation is one-sided, about her. That's what he is interested in that night. She feels like she just woke up one day and found herself adopted by the people here.

Chapter 3

On a television somewhere in Michigan, the report says, "We now join our top reporter in the field covering our latest story that could affect you. Trish."

"Thanks, Sarah! In Saginaw today at the Leah properties, emergency teams were called in action for a mysterious gas leak, forcing many to leave their homes and leaving many more people in critical condition. Victims are being shipped to overflowing local hospitals and nonemergency hubs. The area affected is decreasing in size. The gas causes anyone who comes in contact with it to pass into a coma-like state. Specialists have reported that the gas is so fine, it passes through the protective rubber on the gas masks of rescuers. Three stations of firemen and many officers fell to the gas after a shift in the wind. With carbon monoxide detectors, the backup rescuers have been able to detect the gas and slowly have been saving victims after the gas leaves the area. A large group of young people attending a party were first hit near the center of the outbreak, then it spread to the local homes. Police have discovered that fuel experiments were being conducted in this area but are not certain what the exact cause was because the center is still covered in this suspicious gas. We'll keep you updated. Back to you."

Pictures flash from scene to scene of people lying on the ground. Near the center, there is a large group of people all dressed in firefighter gear lying on top of each other. Further out are the police who had been called in to shut down the party for noise violation. Surrounding houses lie dormant as though it was still midnight. Helicopter camera shots show people being pulled into ambulances and flatbed trucks usually used for hauling larger items. Hospital walls lined with as many patients as possible are being monitored.

* * *

The next day, Nick gets up and looks around the room. It still smells like a woman used to live there. The morning lights the room. It's covered in paisley and looks rather small, but it has its own bathroom but no shower. On the nightstand, he sees a basin with water and soap next to it. He rushes to the door and makes sure it's locked and begins to take a bath. He searches through the drawers and finds women's clothes, some men's clothes his size, money, and a stash of weapons. He belts on a short sword and two knives and notices some books on a shelf. One is labeled *Flame Spirits and How to Enjoy Their Company*. The edges of the pages are blackened as though once on fire. He reaches up and takes it and looks in. On the back of the cover is a label: "Purple tribes books and spells. 234 cir. due back 5 MU 234." Inside, he starts to read the book. It flows like sweet poetry; before he knows it, he has read twenty pages and understood the workings of a starter fire spell. The poem ends with "This is knowledge of ages. Communicate with the elements, and you will go far." He closes the book and looks at the back. There is an address for it in this town.

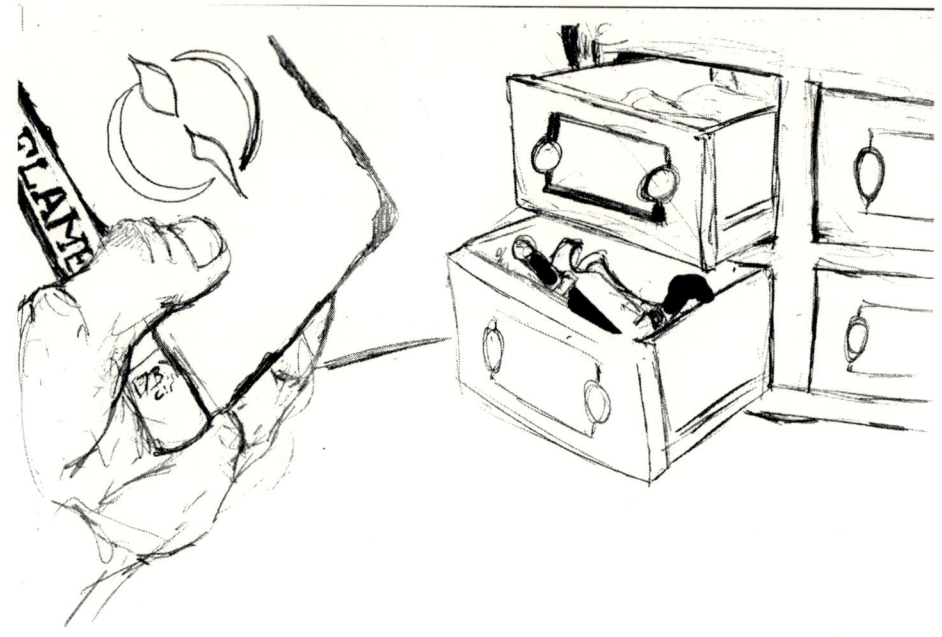

Nick gets up, unlocks the door, goes down the porch, then knocks on Vander's door. He's going to look for a job. He goes downstairs; a woman pig person is there, cleaning with a cow woman and some other animal people.

"Good morning." He smiles at her.

She stands up and wipes her head with the back of her hand. "You must be the new tenant. 'Ope you hang around longer than the other two that left."

"I plan to, but why was he so fast at getting us in?" asked Nick.

"Better to 'ave renters in the rooms than to wait for a new call girl for months. You 'ave to special order them, you know. They are a commodity."

"Well, have a good one. I have to see a man about a book."

"Go to the other end of town. I heard you were new in town and needed a pointer."

"Thanks." Nick winks and heads out.

Everyone is tall compared to him, a feeling he has not felt in years. All he can think of is his body in his past life—tall and skinny, totally different from now. He shakes the feeling, thinking about how he may be able to do magic. Passing through town, he sees many places of business, most usually run by one person. The streets only have a few people walking around. There are a few streets that shoot off the main stretch, but like the woman said, it is literally at the other end of town. The building has three hemispheres and one decorated large cylinder coming out the center. A sign reads Library and Spell Compendium. Nick enters slowly. All the shades are drawn; only streaks of light break through

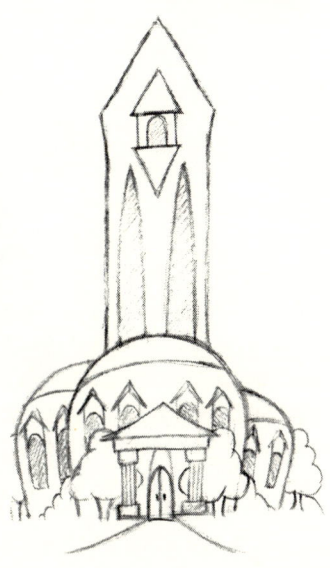

the windows. "Hello?" Nick calls into the tower. Through the alley of fifteen-foot bookshelves, one cone of light beams from a desk, lighting the edges of the piles of books and a lump of clothing behind the desk. Nick cricks his neck around the corner more, letting his shoulders pass the doorframe.

"Who's there?" a voice yells out. The lump slides down. Nick opens the door wide and takes a few steps in. "Who's there? It's rude to not answer. I have been hoping for a visitor for some time, and this is what I get? How embarrassing that this is the person who answers my call," the voice yells again as the lump of clothing rounds the corner.

"Um. Hi. I'm Nick, and I would like some information," Nick answers as he looks around and heads in. Books are all unkempt and lying around; cobwebs, dust, and dishes are piled around the shelves.

"Oo. Who who! So information you want? Maybe I should break out, dance, sing. And in the merriment, the particulars will come into focus. So here I go." Nick lays down the book he found, then the slightly hunched Gias pulls off his robes to reveal a flashy suit that sparkles in some places and looks worn in others. A light shines on him. As he starts turning his hands in circles, sparkles start swirling around him, and his suit starts to look new. "This is my purpose, to give you the latest scoop on all the poop. I can be your guide to these books, tried and true" Books start to dance around, rocking back and forth. But the more he sings and moves, the less the light shows. The last of the books start to drag themselves off the shelves, scraping on the ground toward him.

Nick pleads with his hands out. "You don't have to do this. I'm looking for what you have in planar or planetary travel."

The man looks down at him and stops singing. "What? You can do that?" The light's flickers and sparks disappear; he lightly lands on the ground.

"It's really dark in here. How are you to find anything?" He bends down to look at the title. It's hard to read. *The Misadventures of Cho*!

"Have you been to other worlds?" the man asks, bending down, with Nick trying to look in his eyes. "Please, answer me. I want to know how, that is, if you can." He gets on his hands and knees but is still looking into Nick's eyes.

"I am from another world, and I want to get back. I have nothing here but the clothes on my back." The man jumps for joy.

"Oh, so do you want a job? I could use an assistant! But on one condition. You tell me all about the other world and work with me to get there." He throws his arm around him and walks him to his desk. "Every book is about travel, and some describe where the writer have been!"

"How did you make all that happen when I first came in?"

He cricks his neck and furrows his brow. "What do you mean? You're a Gias like me. You should be able to—far much better, considering you're so young."

Nick replies, "I have a secret. I was just turned into this yesterday. So I have no clue what's going on with this body."

"Really? Then welcome. Welcome to the Plane Secon and Planet Oglathorpe. My name is Max, and you're hired! *Now*, put these books back." He sluggishly moves back to the seat and raises his hand. One spark lights up; it seems that nothing happens.

Nick picks up one book and sets it down on a shelf. "It's still too dark in here." The old Gias is mounting pelts and blankets on top of him. Nick puts the book down and looks around. He thought, *I will never find anything like this, but at least I have a job.* He walks over to a window; it's all boarded up as though it is condemned. He reaches up and touches the oval-shaped board and pulls on it. No give. He pulls it again harder. He climbs up to the top of it and pulls harder, grinding his teeth a bit. He falls to the ground. When he opens his eyes, he notices a symbol on the board. He rubs his finger on it. The door reminds him of the book he just brought in. "Hey! Do you have that book I brought in?"

Standing behind him, the old Gias smiles. "There is a foretelling of two who will come and save the planet from a tyranny that keeps us underfoot without our knowledge. They will face many trials. But first, they have to learn how to be." He hands him the book that he brought in. "For every window I open, I will give you a new book about world travel. I have one for every window. Your task is set . . . Oh, and clean up this place. It's filthy."

Nick opens the book and looks at the chapters; one is about fire-enchanted doors. The chapter is short; it says that you have to ask permission to open such locks, but you can bypass that and match the intensity of the flame with your own and, therefore, open the lock with your own key. "These spells will keep nonmagic users at bay, but you may need a better trick to keep magicians at bay." He puts down the book and starts to say a prayer that sounds like a murmur. In a few seconds, he reaches out his hand to reveal a flame dancing in his hand. He pushes it forward into the symbol; nothing happens. He pushes harder with his mind. The flame gets hotter; sparks come flying from the sides of his hand. The wood shakes, then starts to roll into a little ball, dropping down and taking the shape of a metal diamond.

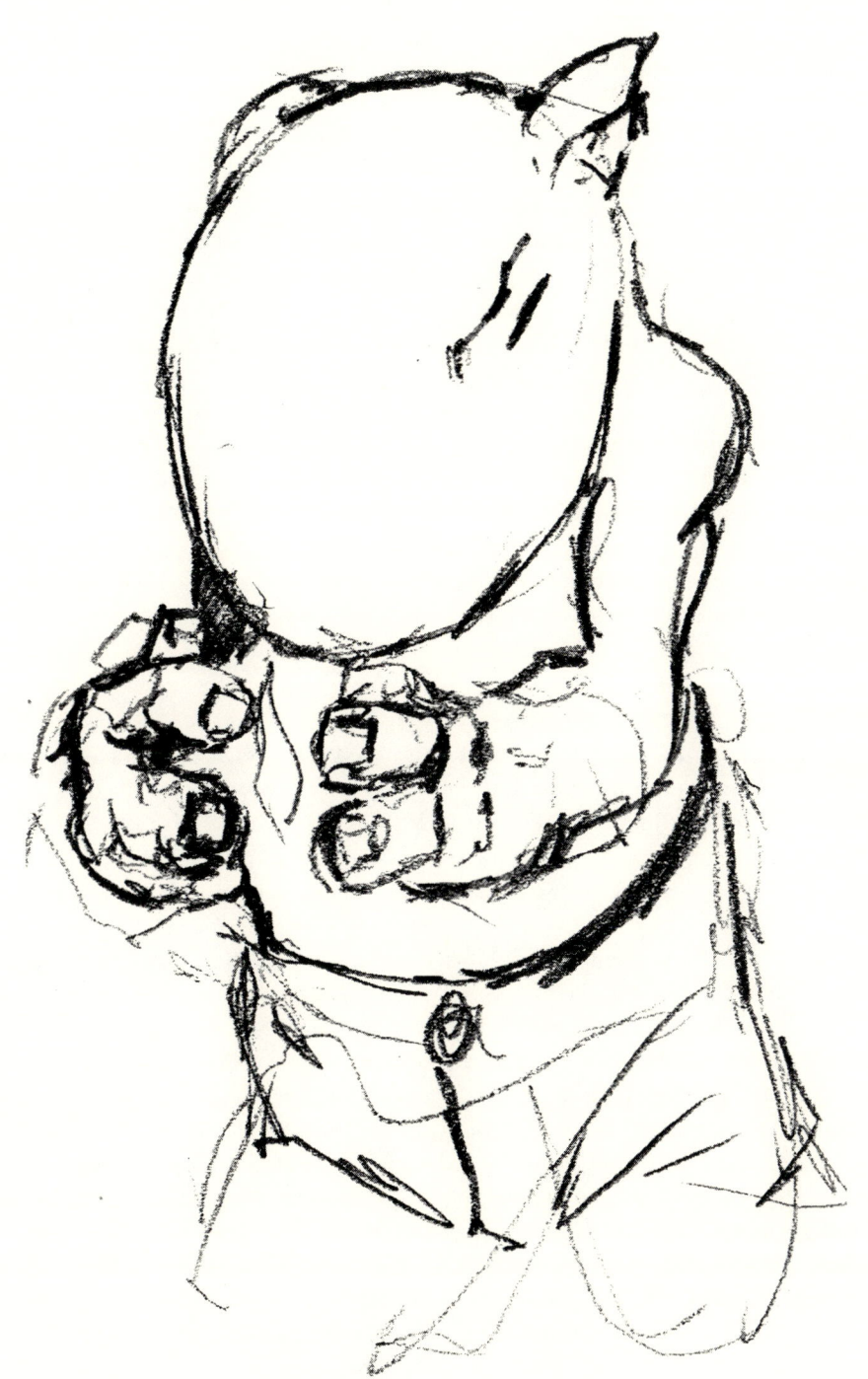

"Wow, my boy, if you're not the chosen one, you're the closest thing to it. I'm Max, the local crazy librarian, or so the townsfolk call me. I have the distinct pleasure of guiding you to your path." Max walks over to the metal shard, picks it up, and stares at it. "Anyone else dropped in here on their second day would never have even made a decent flame." He looks around the portal of light showing the severity of the dust, dirt, and disorganization. "Now, I have that book ready for you to look at, but before you touch it, get to work. I want to see this place look at least 5 percent better before I let you go off with this."

He puts the shard into his pocket and heads back to his chair.

Nick curses under his breath as he noses around. A cleaning closet is in the back by the bathrooms. It is still dark inside; he doesn't even know what he is pulling out. He pours an interesting combination of soaps into a bucket, then a sponge, and drags it out to the lighted area. For the rest of the day, he does as he is asked. The books have a numerical system similar to Dewey decimal, but every book has to be taken off so that the shelves can be cleaned first. By the end of the day, three shelves are cleaned, and Nick is ready to die. Dizzy, he crawls down the case and lies down. Max puts a book in his hand. "Here you go. Good work. Now close up for me, and be back in the morning." Nick watches him through the corner of his eye as he leaves. Nick finishes up and then leaves, closing the door and hanging the Closed sign.

* * *

Vander wakes up, Groggily he rolls out of bed. Stepping over his clothes from last night, his room is quite bare, with only a few pieces of furniture like a mirror, a desk, and of course, the bed. The bathroom is tiny with just a sink and toilet seat. He feels lucky that they have even that since it looks like a town from the Wild West. He starts to wash up with one of the three clothes that he sees sloppily hanging on his rack. *Ping... Ping... Ping.* He hears a noise in the background. He isn't sure what the noise is. It continues, and he becomes interested. He gathers his clothes and gets dressed. He heads out and goes to Nick's room. *The door is closed. He must be sleeping.*

Ping, the sound calls to him. He must know what it is. Heading downstairs, he waves to the working women. As he leaves the saloon, he takes a deep breath, still getting used to animal people. *Ping*—he shakes his head and refocusing, back on track, going the opposite way Nick went, he follows the sound. At nine, windows open automatically as the sun hits more windows. With a little jog in his step, he turns a few corners to find a wide man pounding on a piece of metal. As he gets closer, he notices that the large sac underneath his jaw jiggles after every blow to the metal. Vander approaches slowly. The man only glances up. Vander closes in, feeling awkward but wanting to try. "Nice work." Vander lifts his head like a nod. The man looks at him and squints his eyes and leans over his hot metal.

"Well, boy, it seems that I have piqued your interest, and oddly enough for a human, you come to me. Not too many would think about swinging the hammer." He moves over and lays the metal in the kiln.

Vander moves in. "I have always wanted to try and make something out of metal."

"Against my better judgment, I will let you try. Here is a core. Please show me your skill and make a *U* shoe." He places a piece of ore and a U shoe in his hands at home we would call it a horse shoe. "If you're going to work for me, you have to make this in two hours."

"Well then, I can only try my best." He picks up a hammer and starts to bang away. The blacksmith breathes deeply and watches the boy as he calls him to look down and close his eyes. Vander envisions how it will be done in such a short time. Then he opens his eyes, and he places the ore in the fire. The fat man's eyes widen as he notices that the ore turns red faster than normal. Vander pulls out the ore and starts to hammer a shape. With each blow, the metal flattens out smoothly. Then he folds it, adding powders to prevent oxidation, and continues. In half an hour, he starts to put the bend into it and adds details. Then after fifty minutes of fine-tuning, he cools it off. He places it next to the man with the original one.

He holds up both and compares them. "This will do, but with your skill, I may not be able to pay you for years of experience."

"Sir, pay me what you think is fair. This is my first attempt ever. I just thought that is how I want it to look, and I'm glad it turned out as well as it did."

With shock on his face that melts back to a squinty scowl, he says, "You're lucky I found you first. You might have ended up clearing fields. I will give you the strength you need to be successful, Vander."

Taken aback at hearing his name, Vander is not sure if he has introduced himself or not. "I'm sorry. I think I forgot your name."

"Garitol. You never asked. I work here three days a week. My daughter works up top selling the goods. If you know what's good for you, you'll keep your hands off her."

"All right then, what's next!" Vander is happy to have the job and works the rest of the day making shoes, pins, and nails. To him, it was more like baking—get the right ingredients, melt, and fix it up at the end. He is faster than the old man, but the old man makes him move the hammer in certain ways, making his body hurt from using muscles that he swears he never knew he had. Vander is worried that he can't be able to work as a bouncer tonight. Maybe it will be slow. At four, the old man tells him he could hang up his hammer, for the day is done. Vander doesn't see the old man's daughter that day and wonders what a man like that would have produced. After the cleanup, Vander asks, "Where is your daughter? Is she gone?"

"I don't know. She works at the saloon at night and didn't come home yet." Garitol sighs as he goes upstairs. "Come back in two days. I'm sure we will have our hands full that day too."

Vander's stomach growled something fierce, and he headed back to the saloon to eat. "Oh yeah, I hope Nick is all right. I have been here all day and never caught up with him. Crap."

Vander starts to jog to the saloon. He turns the corner and passes four houses. He sees a figure walking toward him. It's Emily. He comes to a slow stop and approaches her.

"Wow, you look dirty. Where have you been all day?" Emily asks. Vander moves in closer and puts his hand on her waist, pulling her in closer.

"Working out, just for you!" He smiles and leans in for a kiss. A few shallow kisses after, he rubs against her, and Emily replies, "I can smell it."

"Sorry about leaving you there. I heard a weird noise and had to go and check it out."

"What was it?"

"It was the blacksmith. I helped him out today, thus the shower in sweat."

"Oh. Well, I'll see you later. I don't work, but I'll visit."

"'Kay then, later it will be. I can't wait."

He jogs back to see Nick just entering himself.

Chapter 4

"I was the first officer on the scene, I was called there to check out a party that all the kids were going too. I thought it was odd that there wasn't much movement on the parking lot. Usually, kids are all around running in and out of parties like this. Kittie corner from the warehouse party was a research building that had only a few lights on in the third floor, but most crucial was that one window was broken, from what I saw. May have been an accident I thought. I'll make an announcement and have them turn themselves in and just pay for the window. The funny thing is, the closer that I get to the building, the itchier my throat gets. I went around to the side of the building, and a back door was open. My throat really itches. I'm going to get some water. Kids! Kids piled on top of each other, blocking the doorway! What is going on? I push them off each other. I get to the third one when it starts to get dark. I stumbled back a few steps, coughing. Need to call it in. Two more steps, I fall to my knees. Grab my throat and my body goes limp."—Officer Carlos Rossi's statement to Vander and Nick as he passed through the town.

* * *

The saloon is starting to get exciting; people, or rather, animal people start to fade into existence as they move in from out of the city, swaying back and forth like lost souls coming in for judgment. Some go straight home; others move around town for things that they need for the next day. Very few come straight into the saloon. The lights around town are still off.

Nick looks over at Vander. "Oh shit. Hey, man, sorry I haven't been back. I got a job, and he made me work right off the bat."

Vander puts up his hand. "I was busy too. I helped a blacksmith and was gone all day too." He pushes open the door. "Let's get something to eat."

Vander walks up to the bartender. Nick sits down at the table. As minutes pass by, Vander brings two bowls over. Nick asks, "What is this stuff?"

"No reservations." Vander sits down and picks up his spoon. "Very rare cuisine." He takes a bite and nods his head. "Not too bad. I was thinking today as I pounded out that steel that it's been two days and we are still here. Do you think this is like purgatory for all the planets?"

"No," Nick says, taking a bite of food. "I don't think we are dead. Besides, why would we change shape? Well more in me and less in you, I liked being tall."

"Maybe someone took two dehumidifiers and pointed them at each other and boom, a temporal vortex that sucks everything in."

"All right, Occam's razor."

"Ooh, big words."

"Ha-ha. I read once about a theory of the evil deceiver, where the devil or some facsimile is tricking us, pulling a veil over our eyes."

"No, because that is really broad for Occam. First we have to prove that there is this devil and that he has some sort of power over us. Then how do we prove it to others?"

"What if we simplify it to man as the devil and that we are in an experiment, so we are not sure about what is going on?"

"Closer, but still, no. Why us? Usually, there is a reason or a condition to be met to be picked for a science experiment. And if this is a . . . a . . . an animatronic ride, where did they get the AI? Plus not to mention the shape changing!"

"You seem upset about your new look."

"Man, don't cross that road."

"Why, because I would get there twice as fast as you!" Vander laughs a little.

"If you're going to keep going on, then I'll leave."

Vander stands up, holding out his hand. "No, wait, I'm sorry. Let's continue."

"Fine then, continue your drab thoughts on our situation."

"Maybe then it's an evil plant pollen that has taken control."

"Why does everything have to be evil? What if it's just an accident?"

Vander shrugs his shoulders. "Eh, evil just sounds cooler. It makes us sound like we are fighting for the good of everyone here."

"Please, like you're some kind of hero. Here, so save the day. You can't even beat me at board games without cheating. How are you going to beat a major villain?"

"Ah, but I beat you!"

"Hey, you want to piss me off more? You'll remind me of that day again, and this time, I'll do more than throw the board!"

"All right, again, for the twelfth million time, I am sorry and will never be the banker again."

"Let's get past that. I went to the library and got a job putting away books. They have a wide variety of magic books. Might as well learn and use what we can."

"Cool. How easy is magic?"

"It comes down to who has magic and who doesn't. The funny thing is, everyone has the ability. It's all in how you use it. If you take the time to learn and practice, you can become one of the greats."

"Let me guess, you want to be one of the greats."

"Hey, we have been here for two and a half days. We have no signs that we can leave and even less of a sign that we are going back anytime soon. So why not try and learn what goes on here and take advantage of it?"

"Do you think I have the power to use magic?"

"I can't tell. The only thing that I am sure of is that what I turned into is naturally endowed with magic. So even if you are magically powered, I'm sure that I will be able to learn faster than you!"

"Oh la di da. You know how to take any disadvantage and turn it one-eighty."

"*Sí*, exactly. Looks like your shift's about to begin. The boss hog is staring at you."

"Yeah, well, take it easy tonight, find a girl, and relax. We never know when it will be time to go. In fact, I see someone checking you out over there." At the end of the bar is a woman taking two drinks and winking at him.

Hm, that was easy, Vander thinks to himself. *Aw, I have known her for only a few hours, but I miss Emily.*

Vander gets up and walks to the door. It is his turn to watch for weapons. Nick pulls back a chair and starts talking. This will be an easy night. He is right. Everyone comes in and just wants a drink this night. It gets even easier, seeing that Emily comes to visit him only an hour later. They chat up a storm about the local happenings.

Vander finds out more about Joe and Joeism. It turns out that someone founded Joeism two thousand years ago. And guess what his name was. In his religion he was the be-all and end-all. So Joe was a savior to the land of chaos. He lived for 150 years, performed miracles, set up governments and guards, then disappeared. But fifty years later, someone just like him showed up. He looked just like him and had the same ideals and motives. He ran like a system checkup, making sure that his beliefs and works were all kept intact. That person fought his way back to the top, although by killing thousands that did not follow in his steps. He ruled for sixty years and then disappeared—again. Every time he shows up the story seems to start over but in a different part of the island, where ever there is the most prosperity he appears there. The most disturbing part is that life without him is usually really nice. Now one of the most interesting things that he finds out is that humans have only been here roughly a thousand years. This is eye-opening material to process.

Vander had been going through his memories to think of what was the last time he could remember. He is thinking that if man had only been around for a thousand years, then what brought them here? Not to mention, why the rarity of seeing man? His memory keeps coming down to a poster that everyone crowded around to see, and a party where everyone was panicking. Across the room is a man putting up a poster for Winter Ball 2004. Vander looks down, shakes his head, then looks back at the poster—a warehouse colored with all the funky and neon glow—as the man puts it up, tacking it in place. Then in the middle of that thought, Emily breaks him out of his stare. The poster is for a fortune teller, Crystal Ball Zoey, and the warehouse is a wagon being pulled by a giant purple cat. "Next week Tuesday, you and I are going on a picnic." Emily smiles at him. Vander looks down at her and agrees. He goes back to work, watching people for weapons. Emily gives him a kiss. "Now don't work too hard, killer!" His shift ends, and they take it upstairs. Even though it has already been two days, he wants to make sure that he doesn't want to wake up with regrets. In the doorway, he leans in and kisses her. She opens the door and leads him in. She leaves and goes back to her house in the morning.

Chapter 5

"Underfunded and poorly equipped, I *am* surprised that I'm still alive after all the accidents." A man in a white suit mixes liquids together. His protective helmet is covered in spots, and the face shield is splattered. "How do they expect me to find the new miracle fuel when I can't even get a new, clean face guard?" *Achoo!* He knocks over all the things on his desk. "Ah, damn it, I can't even see!" He stumbles around, feeling his way out, walking fast. *Bam!* He hits a shelf, knocking it over. Liquids start spilling out and mixing together. "My suit is getting wet. What is going on? I can't breathe." He backs up, pulling down his mask to see past his filthy mask. He slips on a test tube and lands in the liquid. He starts to burn and stands up staring at his hands. In a panic, he starts to instinctively reaching in a panic as his eyes feel they are about to swell out of his head. He lands on some barrels that he carelessly left open tumbling them over mixing more of the liquids. "I can't breathe!" In a moment of insanity his eyes focus and he see a window, he bolts to the window, unable to see his distance to it he crashes into it shattering it to a million pieces.

He tumbles through the hole, shards of glass tearing his suit to bloody shreds and falling three stories.

*   *   *

Emily feels that today is going to be one of the greatest days in her life. She wakes up early, humming out her thoughts. The sweet song carries her as she makes breakfast for the family. She sends her dad off to the smith shop and her mother off to the market. She cannot stop thinking about how perfect her plan for the day is going to be. Today is the day that she is going to prove her love for him and show him that she can take care of him. She packs a basket with bread, meat and some seasonings. She takes along a soft blue blanket, her favorite.

She carries the basket with both hands, wearing a nice spring dress that flows with the wind. Dust kicks up with every step. She makes her way to the saloon. The cleaning ladies are hard at work scrubbing away food and drink. Light seeps in through the windows in the upper deck. She walks up the stairs, avoiding the creaks although proving it pointless with the chattering of the old women. The number 3 door is old and faded. Emily turns the handle, which is locked. Emily pulls out an old key, long with a block-shaped end. The key is the master key for the saloon. Part of the plan is a success; she has access to what she wants. She slides the door open. The room is dark; not too much light seeps in. Vander lies sleeping on his bare chest and is barely covered with his blanket. Laying down the basket next to the door, she slowly stands back up, cautiously making sure the conditions are right. She dashes forward. *Thud, thud.* The woman leaps into midair, arms reaching forward. *Bam!* The bed legs break, sending them across the room. Dust flies in a giant cloud. Vander's eyes bulge out. She sits up on his lap, smiling from ear to ear. Vander lies back. "I saw you coming."

"Through the back of your eyelids? I don't think so!"

He reaches up and grabs her by the arms, rolling her over, then getting on top. "Haven't you heard of 'that's too early'?"

"Nope! It's never too early for a loving, good morning jumping!" She smiles and giggles at him. "Now get ready, you just woke up."

"Hold on, I have to get ready. I just woke up." Then he looks confused. "It's official. You know me too well."

Later, after washing up and walking Nick to work, Vander and Emily continue out of town, carrying the basket full of goodies.

"I'm glad that you landed here for a while. I thought I would have to go on some kind of mystical journey to find a soul mate."

Vander stops walking and stares into Emily's eyes. "You think that we are soul mates?"

She grinned. "Why does that scare you? I can take it back."

Vander replies with a grin. "You can't take that back. I heard it, and you can just change your mind from soul mate to boyfriend again. I think that it's great. I just never thought that I would have someone call me that. Even from the person I would be marrying."

"Really? That's great! I have felt so lonely here in this town. Even with all the people here, no one looks at me like you do."

"What, like this?" He raises his eyebrow and looks through the corner of his eye. "Or . . ." He then crosses his eye and makes his lips protrude and wiggle. Emily laughs and puts her hand on his chest. He then takes her into his arms and gives her a kiss. "I'm sure that no matter what happens, we will make it for the long run."

A caravan rolls over the hill that they are about to go over. The main cart is being pulled by a giant purple cat. Vander looks again. It is the one from the poster on the wall. It has a rounded roof, and the reins go inside of the cart. The front wheels go all the way up the sides, almost touching the roof, then thirty feet back are the little wheels. The cart is segmented and rolls smoothly over the ground, as though it can actually glide across. It has many markings carved into it. Some he has seen in Nick's books; most are for protection, and some are spells for attack. Emily pulls him to the side, saying that they have reached where she wants to eat. She has not recognized the cart; she has been waiting for them to come for three weeks now. Vander is helping to smooth out the blanket when he suddenly feels a hot breath of air roll over his shoulders. Emily laughs as she watches Vander turns around to a giant cat licking him all over his face. He makes funny faces after, like he is mortified.

A door in the middle of the long cart opens, and a woman comes out first. She is a short old insect woman. "I am sorry, he must smell something he likes—foodwise,

that is. Why is he being so lovey on you?" Vander looks over at her with his mortified face. "I'm Zoey, the fortune-teller."

"I know, I'm so glad to meet you. I was going to see you as soon as you made camp." Emily's eyes grow bigger the more she talks.

"Why wait? Come on in, the two of you, I shall tell you your fortunes. It sounds like we were destined to meet." She steps back inside, leaving the door open.

Emily opens the basket, pulling out a sweet meat. The cat sits up and puts its paws in the air. The cart jerks into the air, the door slams back, and a scream comes from the inside. The cat lands and sulks down, realizing what it has done. Emily laughs and feeds it the sweet meat.

She knows that Vander is jealous. That is his favorite food he found here. She pulls his hand and leads him into the cart. The room looks messy, maybe to add mysticism to the whole show. The woman is on her back with her feet kicking in the air; she screeches for help. Emily runs over and helps the woman to her seat. Zoey kicks around, looking like she's trying to jump up at the same time.

"Eh, eh . . . eh!" She grunts as she rolls up. "Mmm. Now let's see. We're all meant to do something. Sometimes great, sometimes small that builds to a great. Hold out your hands." She hacks a loogie into her hand. Emily's face turns from enchantment to twisted, utter disgust. "Ah look, you'ra in real love now, not like the last one who had his way and left you. That was a quickie for sure. You'ra destiny is going to get others in your path moving forward, hopefully not to this swirly here." She takes her finger and mixes it up. "Seems a way out, *but* not likely."

How the Hell Do We Get Home From Here?

Outside, there is a figure riding a giant beast. The beast seems to lunge forward with every step, lifting its heavy hands, hovering it over the ground for a few feet, and letting it land heavy. The body narrows down toward the legs, looking powerful enough to push over a mountain. Its head swings low with every step. The figure looks on to see the city not far off and, even closer, a small caravan. The figure slides off the back, a ten-foot drop. The figure looks to the left and right. She waves her hands and holds out certain fingers with certain gestures. A fire starts out and burns around the monster. The monster looks down in sheer panic. It starts to panic and rears, landing extra heavily, charging forward, shaking all the trailers in the caravan.

Inside the caravan, the woman finishes up with a speech on true love and to remember it always. She spits a bigger pool in Vander's hand. "You, my big friend, are a hero." The caravan starts to shake. The caravan starts to pitch and toss items around, covering the pillowed floor. The cat outside screams and jerks the cart. Vander pulls Emily and the old lady up out of the piles of pillows and junk. Emily watches as Vander takes off toward the monster. Then Zoey grabs Emily's arm. "I told you he was a hero."

Emily turns to her. "I'll be right back. I have to keep up." Leaving everything there, she starts to run after them both. The monster pauses, letting out a great scream. Dust billows as a bird takes flight all around. Vander starts gaining ground, running as fast as he can. Bam Bam, the monster, lands its two massive feet, shaking the ground. Vander gets to its side. He waves his arms in the air, yelling, "Hold on, big fella!" Having never seen a beast this big other than on movie screens, he takes a step back as the monster swings his head toward him. Emily catches up with him. "Watch out!" She shoves him out of the way as a giant hand the size of a tree trunk crashes beside him, just missing his legs. It opens its mouth and lets out a scream, sounding more terrified than offensive. It looks forward again and lifts its far hand. Vander gets to his feet, grabbing on to its other hand. The beast is hot and sweaty. Slowly he starts to climb, gripping tighter every time the monster lands it foot. Emily reaches to help and climbs on but is pulled back by the figure.

She falls and looks up. Rachel, the figure, lets the wind blow away the concealing shawl. Rachel stands, pulling Emily up. She is slender, letting her curves show through the protective gear she wears. The shawl blows away before she can grab it. Her face is plain, and her hair has a red tinge to it. "I thought you would be gone forever!" Rachel pulls her up. "Take me to your home, fast. I need to hide! They are after me, and I have a plan to get them off my trail."

"So you're going to kill off the town to do it!" Emily yells angrily.

"No." Rachel grabs Emily's hand, pulling her with her. "He's really kind. He'll just run through town and cause a little ruckus. We'll slip in, and I'll hide in the cellar."

"Wait, who are you running from? I thought you left to go get rich."

"The crimson guard. I found out that I could do magic and use it to help me get my fortune. I left it in the last town."

They start to run. "You can do magic? How did you find out?"

"Not now—later. He won't be the longest distraction."

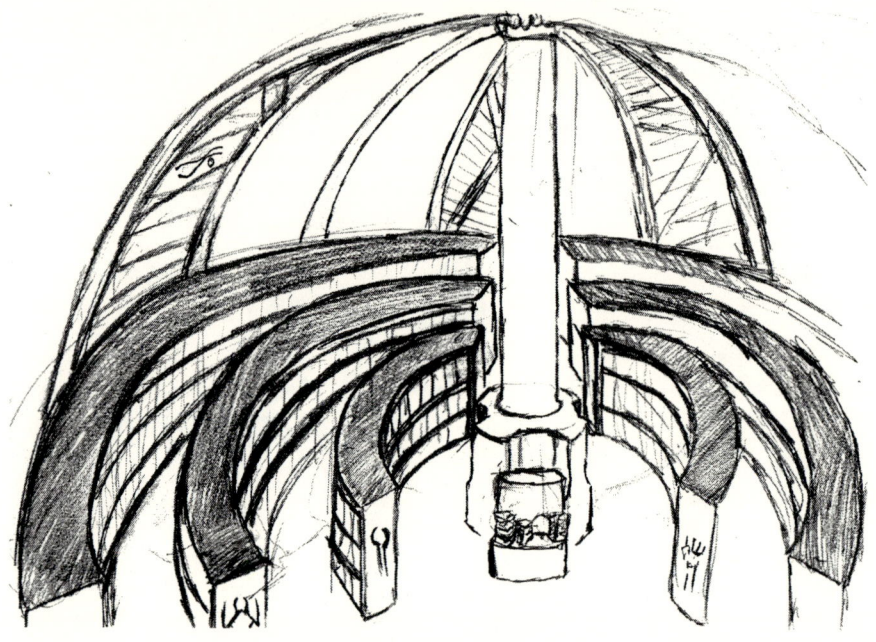

Nick's job for the day is to clean the shelves. He figures out another window, letting in much more light and exposing the years of dirt on top of the shelves. Then two hours later, he was yelled at about the water being too dirty and needing to be changed. "Fifteen minutes of song and dance to tell me that I *need* to change the water. Nice crescendo." The only hard part was taking the water to the road; it had to be lifted the whole way. "I like it, but man, I could go one whole day without hearing a lame song about how things work or how I'm messing up." Nick looks to his right; a huge cloud of smoke is racing its way toward him. Loud, thudding noises seem to come from inside the cloud. He thinks to himself, *I should get inside so I don't get dirty. But what the hell is that?* Finally, he sees the monster. "Damn, I guess I'll go in now." With a second look, he sees that the monster has a huge shadow moving up its side, almost getting ready to ride. "I bet it's him. If not, then I would like to see who it is."

How the Hell Do We Get Home From Here?

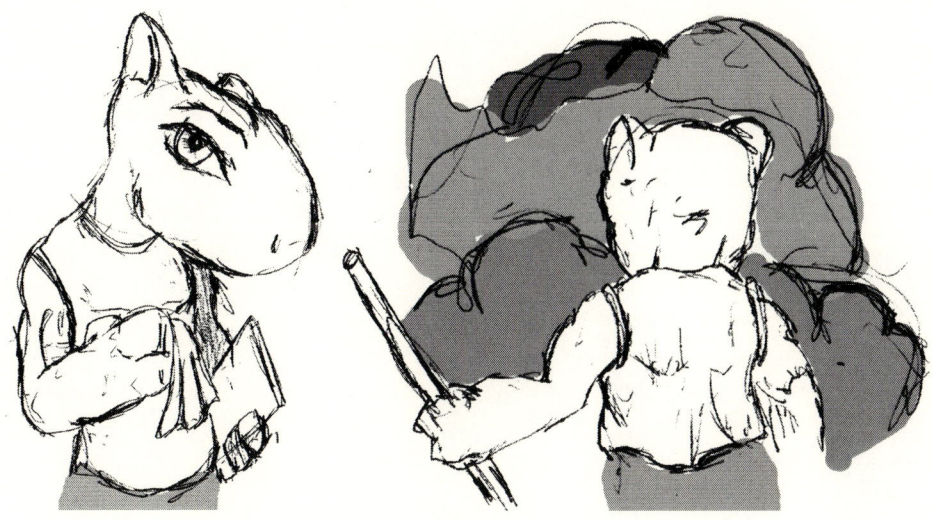

A straining voice comes from the cloud. "Nick, help me!" Nick starts to run. It's only a matter of seconds before he jumps on and sees the situation. Vander gets to the top, grabbing a rein. He leans to the side and picks up Nick.

"So how was your day?" Vander yells back.

"Not as exciting as yours!" Nick yells to him.

Vander looks around and grabs the monster all over. Nick stares ahead, watching the town get larger. "So do you have a plan, or are we going to get blamed for this!"

"Hey, use your magic and freeze his head or something."

"Ah hell, why not!" He climbs over Vander and uses him as a brace. Vander's face is buried into Nicks back. Nick moves his hands and starts an incantation. The air around them gets colder. The monster's face starts to ice over like frost on a branch. "It's no use. The ice needs to gather in one place for it to be really effective." The town is getting closer; animal people start to take notice as they run by. Vander pulls back on the reins as hard as he can, digging his heels into its neck. Nick grabs one, pulls the monster's head, and moves to the right slightly. Nick sees a huge rock up ahead. He swings off the beast and lands with a roll.

"Nick!" Vander yells. He grabs the right rein and stands on its neck, pulling as hard as he can and moving its head more to the side. Nick starts another spell. The rock seems to move and roll onto the road. The monster can't see it and collides with it at full speed, pushing the rock like a plow. The earth is mounded around, clearly leaving a trail where the beast had fallen. The sudden stop throws Vander off the beast. He hits the stone and rolls down. Dirt covers him for the last stretch. Nick runs over and starts digging him out. Some of the locals run over to help.

Emily and Rachel run past the field next to the commotion. Emily sees Vander bleeding slightly and tries to stop it. Rachel doesn't let go of her. She whispers, "Damn it, this ruins my easy passage into town."

How the Hell Do We Get Home From Here?

People from the town come running to check on things after a loud crash like that. Rachel, staying low, says, "Maybe not. It may just be enough." They sneak in through the outskirts of the town, running fast from house to house until they reach Emily's house.

"Now can I check on him?" Emily says with concern.

"No, they will wonder why you came from this way. Please hide me and then go back to the caravan and come back to town that way."

"Okay, but we are going to have to talk when this is over."

"Deal."

Emily moves a trunk into the middle of the room, then picks up a chair and lays that on top. She reaches up to a knot in the ceiling. She pulls down a rope and opens the door and rolls out some stairs. Rachel climbs up; she rolls up the stairs and pulls the rope up.

"I will bring you food after dinner." Emily leaves and moves around town, heading back to Vander. She sees the monster lying on its side, still breathing. The animal people gather and help him sit up. Nick's glowing hand makes the cuts close up slowly but surely. Emily runs up and pushes past a couple of people. Vander looks up. "What happened? I thought I saw you catching up."

"I am way out of shape. I kept up as long as I could but then you were busy trying to climb that thing." She moves over and hugs his head. "I'm sorry, baby. I was just trying, and I couldn't keep up."

"It's okay, you don't need to fight the bad guys with me. Just be there for me to kiss you. Ouch!" Vander reacts to being poked in a wound by Nick.

People move back as a caravan approaches. Lady Zoey rolls up; the cat starts sniffing Emily. The side of the wagon is all muddy. Nothing was broken.

Emily, with her mouth covered, asks, "Are you all right? I should have stayed and helped."

"Hunay, you'ra fine. My menz helped and got us back and running." She then looked up to the crowd. "This wasn't an accident. Someone was trying to show you a sign! Danga is coming."

Chapter 6

A newspaper clipping says,

"Yesterday, a breakout of a poisonous gas spread through an industrial area and a local residence till 6 pm. An evacuation of all local area occupants is still in effect till 11 pm tomorrow. A total of Three hundred fifty three people have been sent to hospitals, among them mostly teens. Hospitals are having trouble finding places to store all the patients. Symptoms of the patients are coma and redness around the eyes. Although in this coma, some of the patients have muscle spasms and seem to be dreaming. The fuel company expresses its sympathy to the families and will fully fund finding a cure.

* * *

    Another month and a half go by. Nick and Vander keep a vigilant eye for any clues as to how they got there. They even watch out for more humans; none has arrived since them—not even passed through town. The barkeep says, "This isn't the most popular town. We are deep in the peninsula that many people pass right by. This seems to be the only town around that old people do not come to die in." Nick finds a teleportation spell, but it was limited to them because they had to have been there once to go back. They popped all over town before they figured that one out. The townspeople start to enjoy themselves as the caravan opens up and brings rare goods, games, and hand-built rides. Lady Zoey is the main attraction. People line up for hours to hear what could happen. Some are fast almost in and out; others stay for more than an hour during their readings.
    Vander is worried about Emily. She has started to act weird after that day. Some days, she is flaky; and on others, she doesn't want to even leave the bed. It frustrates Vander on the days that she is distant and will not give him a sign of anything. Yesterday, she left him at work, saying, "How do you think you would feel if someone you loved was wanted dead?" Vander thinks about his family. What would he do if they were wanted dead. What if he is wanted and he didn't know it? Vander will do all he can to help him clear their name or stop the hunt. What bothers him more is, who is she talking about? Who is on a hit list?

Nick is up late studying. His light is on when Vander comes upstairs. Just as he would do on any night that Nick had his light on, he pokes his head in.

"Hey there."

"Hey, what's up?" Nick asked.

"Do you know what's up with Emily?"

"Well, with your tongue constantly down her throat, I'm surprised you know what her voice sounds like."

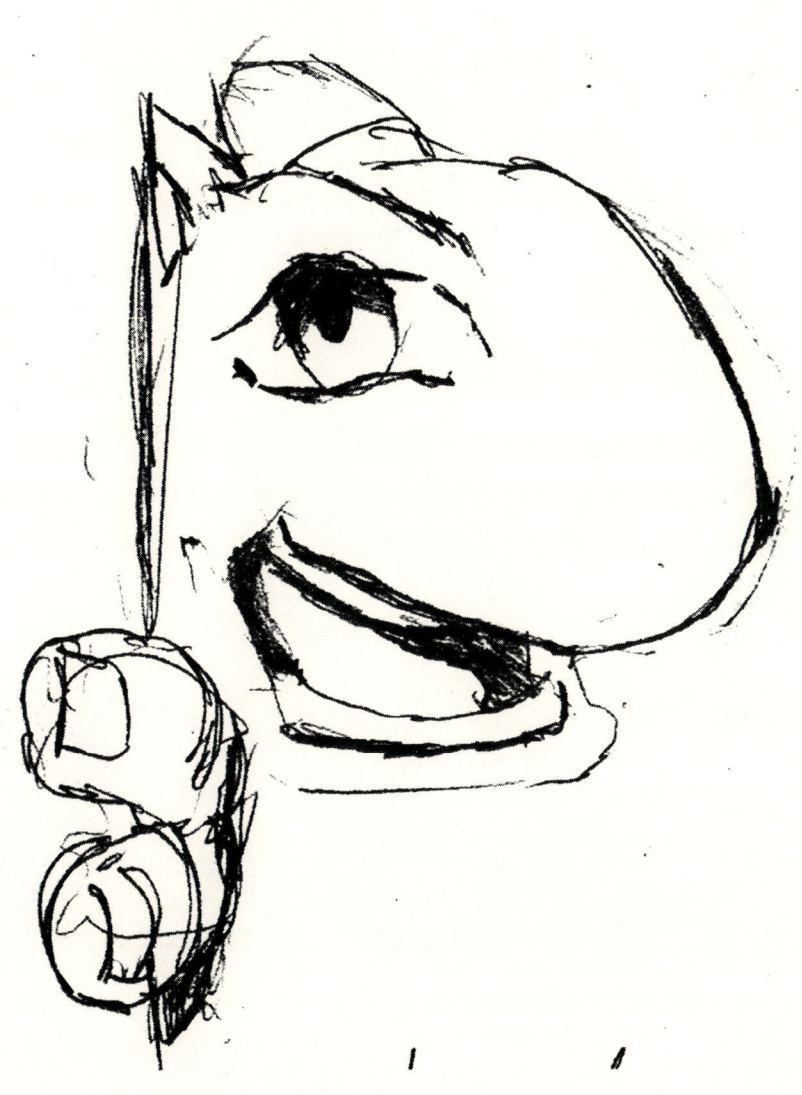

"Ha-ha. Well, I just thought that she might say something to you. We do hang out almost every morning."

"She has changed since that day. Maybe she wants to break up with you and doesn't know how to. There aren't a lot of humans to choose from around here. I'd take her, but look, it's kinda awkward."

"I know, you're so small."

"No, jackass. I'm talking about being with my best friend's girl."

"Oh, thanks, that would suck."

"Pick up that book. I need help studying for combat magic."

"Wow, you're moving pretty fast in this stuff!"

"I really am surprised that you're not. This is like a dream come true. It's real. Not a stupid card game."

"Well, work and girls take a lot too. Besides, check out these biceps." He leans in and kisses one.

"Dude, don't you need to wash before you do that? I'm about to finish this new spell. Take a look"

"What is it?"

"Well, you're supposed to move your hands and say *stosaya*."

Vander hears the wood crackling. He jumps up and looks back. The chair has turned to stone as finely carved as the chair was. "Wow, looks like it works." He sits back down.

Vander cracks open a book. "Okay, question one." Vander starts to question Nick using the book of the written test. They stay up for a few more hours with Nick getting most of the questions right. After the lamp goes out, they call it quits. They only go out after hours of use.

Nick gets up and piles his books on the bed to take them back to the library. He asks for help usually, but he and Vander were up pretty late. He runs to the library; the librarian waits for him and opens the door. "Come on in before it gets too late."

Nick looks at him in puzzlement. "Late for what?"

The librarian grabs him by the shoulders and looks at him with a gleam in his eyes. "This is one of the last things I can teach you before you move on. Lady Zoey is about to leave, and I have a prediction to fulfill."

"You people here are full of nonsense. How can you believe that one person can tell the future for everyone? I can't even tell the future for myself."

The librarian floats to the top of the shelves. "Come on up if you can." He is humming a tune, something like Mozart but different.

Standing at the bottom with hands to his hips, he says, "Come on, old man, you know I can get up there. It would be a lot easier if you taught me how to fly." He takes hold of the shelf and starts up the ten-tier shelving. The old man sits at the top as Nick gets to the top and swings his leg over, rolling up. "You're not going to make me clean up here, in case of a special inspection."

"No, but that is a good idea. You never know." Max rubs his chin.

"Now, whoa . . ." He looks, and all the plain work that was there when he cleaned it is gone, and a nicely finished wood with design burned into it lies before him. "These are all the spells that I learned so far."

Max smiles. He starts to spin and dance, shooting his leg out periodically, then changing it up, flailing his arms around like a dancer in a Broadway show. "Do you know why you didn't cast that spell two months ago? When the monster attacked, you tried and came close, but no go on the spell." He bends low, then floats in the air, balls up then bursts out his arms and legs; and a ball of flame shoots out from him, almost hitting Nick. Nick leaps back just before it hits him.

"What the hell, man?" Nick angrily replies.

"Spells can be cast on the move. Many do not know this. To cast a spell while you're moving takes concentration and a focus weapon." Max pulls out a wand, not very long, and it is taped to his arm. Max yelps as he pulls it off. "I wish that the pain was predicted." It is beautiful; it is made of three twisted pieces: one is wood, one is glass and the other is metal. Each one has a inscription down the middle and is six inches long. "The wand doesn't need to be fancy. One of the most impressive was a twig picked up off the ground. Here, try this first." Max throws Nick a very straight piece of wood. "The first task is to tunnel through the wand and imagine a line to the other object. Then it will be affected. It'll take some time."

Nick looks it up and down. "Nice!" He stands in a heroic stance and points the stick. It flies from his hands past Max and pierce the pillar in the middle of the room. Max floats over and wiggles it out.

Max shrugs his shoulders as he gives it back. "Hold on to it and picture a spell." Nick squints his eyes, holding the wand tight. He thinks the floor is on fire. He sees a flame, and it starts to grow.

"I think I got it!" Nick yells in pleasure. Then he raises his other hand and spreads his fingers. The fire spreads all over and looks as though gasoline has just been lit and has covered the whole ground. He then flips his hand over and moves it up. The flame comes off the ground. He closes his fist, and the flame starts to ball up. A clapping comes from under them. Lady Zoey floats to the top.

"I knew that you had it in ya."

"What are you doing here?" Nick asks with concentration and a slight hint of disgust.

"I'm here to help you flesh this out." She lands on the case next to them. She waves her hand, and an entire field of flowers open on the shelf around her. "You should dust more."

"I know, but the sweeter side of the binding got to me, and it was till this boy came to me that I got my true sense of self back." Max changes from a flamboyant librarian to more of his true educated self, more self confident with a strong presence. Nick notices right away; if this is going to be the new game, then he has to step up his game.

"Now walk around me and cast an ice spell. Make it a simple one so that we don't end up having to thaw out all night." Nick moves his hand as he walks, making shapes in the air. He puts his hands out. Shards start to form in front of his hand. In a swift action, he sends the ice ball straight to Max. Max puts out his hand, deflecting the spell to the side. Nick is astonished. He didn't know that spells could be deflected. Hell, he didn't even know he could cast spells on the move.

Max says, "There are two ways to make a spell stop or to deflect it. To stop it, you have to know what spell is coming at you and to cast that same spell to neutralize it. The easier way is to deflect it. This technique took years to develop and was almost lost after magic had faded in this world. For hundreds of years, we found as many books as we could to rebuild our knowledge."

Max walks over to Nick, leans over, and whispers into his ear. Nick runs to the other side and readies himself. Max looks over to Lady Zoey; they smile and look at each other. They start to move their hands in tiny discrete movements. They start to run at him. Lady Zoey starts to float and launches her attack. Hundreds of fire balls fly at Nick. Max stomps heavily. The beautiful wooden floor splinters, rolling toward him. Nick starts a spin. He throws his hand up, deflects the fire, then swipes away the rolling wood, leaving bubbles in the middle. Lady Zoey jumps over to Max and Nick's shelf, slashing down with a sword made of flame. Nick

How the Hell Do We Get Home From Here?

rolls over the bubble just in time. Zoey doesn't think twice to swipe across, burning halfway through the wood. Nick puts his hands out with the wand and just thinking the words, and the flame disappears. Max runs up, pulling Nick back.

"Are you crazy!" She pushes out her hand, sending Nick through the air. She shoves Max over the edge. He starts to float; she holds out her hand and calls the spell canceling his, sending him plummeting to the ground. Nick lands at the other end, screeching to a halt. He puts his hands up to his head then to the ground, lifting himself up. Lady Zoey screams and runs to him. Nick feels cold running all around him. Nick casts the first level of ice. The spells clash, spilling over each other. Slush sprays over them both. The balls of energy blow up in front of them. Nick rushes in and tries to kick her knees. She notices and yells, "This is a magic war!" She jumps up, and the wood starts to bubble up at him again. This time, he has no real reaction time and is rolled almost over the edge. Wood splinters hit him in the face like hundreds of fists hitting him in the face. Nick holds his hands out in a star shape and yells, "Speak ease no more!"

Lady Zoey looks at him, holds out her hands, and tries to curse him. Nick flinches; he knows what is coming. Nick, in a second, then realizes that the specific spell needs to be yelled. She casts the flame sword again and raises her hand. Nick jumps up and touches her elbow. "Stosaya." Lady Zoey brings her arm down; the blade dissipates. She holds her arm close to her as if in extreme pain, then falls to her knees. Nick puts his hand on her head and starts chanting, "Dia dia *dias*!" A light seemingly from heaven comes down and surrounds them. A dark shadow falls to the ground, holding on to her for dear life. Nick points at it. "Figia!" The shadow burns to a cinder and lies on the ground. Lady Zoey takes a deep breath and rubs her hands against her eyes, then plops down on the ground.

Max climbs to the top. Nick readies to fight. Max yells, "Stop! She is being controlled by something!" Breathing heavily, he says, "Oh, good chap." Going back to his odd, sweet self, he says, "Assess the situation, and strike just like I taught you." Nick and Lady Zoey both look at him funny.

"I can see into the past too. I usually keep that stuff to myself, and it helps me predict what someone will do better." She carries her arm heavily. It has been turned to stone up to her shoulder. "I'm glad you're on to being a full-strength wizard yet, or I would have to go to the masonry instead of my tent."

Nick, looking battered from the fight, walks over to her and sits down. "What was that—that black thing?"

Lady Zoey waves her hand; flowers start to grow all around her and Nick. "Nick, I have not read your future, for you can go many ways. I would hate to see me picking my favorite path for you and having a bad effect on your life. You are a hero, no matter what path you pick. I went through your recent futures to see which one would test you the best and the quickest."

"So that monster that was in you had control?" Nick asked.

"No, I had control of him. He just made the suggestions to kill you in the best way. I was riding copilot for a little. I am leaving soon. You need to be ready. And I approve!"

"And hot damn, so do I!" Max said gleefully. He starts to prance around.

Both Nick and Lady Zoey yell, "No songs!" They were both too sore to have Max start a giant dance routine that would involve them.

Lady Zoey stands up. "I actually didn't see this coming. Very strange. I looked into many different possibilities, and the stone spell didn't come up. When did you learn it?"

"Well, if you want to check out the chair up in my room, you'll know!" Nick chuckled.

"Well, get to climbing, you'll learn to float soon enough." Lady Zoey chuckles back. She pulls out a sash from her belt and ties up her arm, then uses the excess to cover herself up. Then she turns and jumps down. Nick looks at Max; he shrugs his shoulders and looks up at him as he floats down. *Damn*, Nick thinks to himself. He turns around; all the bookshelves are fixed. Then he takes a deep breath and rolls off and climbs down. When he reaches the ground, no one is inside the building, but he hears a voice telling him to go outside.

A group of men march into town. They are covered in a dark-red armor; all the pieces are connected by a black cloth. A figure follows; his shoulder-length hair blows in the wind, and a large weapon is strapped to his back. He doesn't move, but his soldiers seem to move as though instinct guides them to ransack all that is in their path. All the people of the town keep their heads down as though not to cause trouble. The figure gets closer to town; he is white, six feet tall with dark-blue eyes. He pulls out a small bag, opens it up, and pulls out a small paper and a clump of dried tobacco, then begins to roll it. Emily turns the corner, coming out from the back of the house and carrying her basket, ready for the market. She waves to Vander walking by; the old man in the back grunts loudly. Not looking where she is going, she bumps into one of the soldiers, knocking him off balance. "Move, wench!" He swings a backhand at her, hitting her and making the basket fly into the air and her fall to the ground. He hovers over her like an animal ready to kill. Vander drops everything and runs over. The soldier doesn't pay attention as he winds up to hit again. Vander leans in and hits the soldier with his elbow, sending him flying into a fruit stand already torn to shreds.

"What's the matter, ass? You can't use your words and say sorry?" Vander grits his teeth, putting his hand down and helping Emily to her feet.

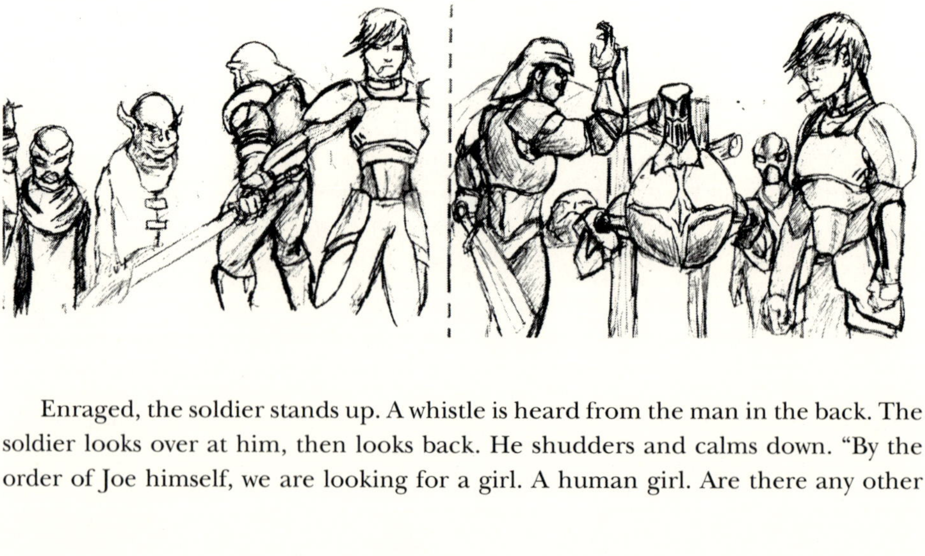

Enraged, the soldier stands up. A whistle is heard from the man in the back. The soldier looks over at him, then looks back. He shudders and calms down. "By the order of Joe himself, we are looking for a girl. A human girl. Are there any other human girls in this town? If so, bring them out so we can verify that they are not the one we are looking for."

Vander shoves him again. "Screw you, you're leaving now!" All the townsfolk start to look up, some worried and others with a renewed sense of pride. The soldier grabs his weapon and pulls it out—a heavy bastard sword with jagged edges. Fred flies over. "Stop! I do not feel her here. There is a great power here somewhere, and it is confusing me. I need to go back and start the tracking again." He puts two fingers in the air. All the guards circle up and start to march out. The soldier looks back before they leave town. "Later, hero."

As they leave, the caravan with Lady Zoey leaves out the other end of town. She sits on the top with a driver and waves to the people as they leave. "Be good, children. I will return!" People start running, blocking the road behind her. Some even start to cry as though something that made them whole is now missing. Children run after her, yelling for her to turn around. "I can't, my babies. I got to help someone else." Nick comes running up to Vander and Emily.

Emily brushes herself off and notices her elbow is bloody. "Since you're new here, let me tell you that was the crimson guard. They used to come around a lot. It's one of the few reasons that we love the war in the east. Keeps them busy. Those bastards are the reason that Rachel left in the first place. They kidnapped people that could use and manipulate magic. One day, we were playing in the grove to the south. We got lost, and it was dark. We gathered wood and tried everything we could think of. Then she turned to the wood, stomped her foot, and yelled for it to light up, and it did. The next day, we were found. People had followed the smoke and caught up with us in no time. Funny part is, we weren't that far away." They start walking back. "They came for a Gias that used to be our friend. Her name was Mishel." She laughs and stops. "Mishel was great. She entertained us for hours. It broke our hearts to see her go in chains. Plus, it was too close to home for Rachel. She was not going to be the next victim, so she ran. I think we need to make a plan and get out of here soon."

Garitol stumbled over. "Thanks for taking care of my daughter. I would have killed him and probably get killed myself! Then how could I take care of my family?"

Vander smiles. "Well, she is my girlfriend. How else should I act?"

Garitol scowls at both of them. Vander looks over at her. "Wait, did I just hear that right? You're her dad?"

Garitol raises his eyebrow. "Stepfather, but still responsible. I knew you were acting funny for the past few weeks, but I didn't know it was because of him."

Vander rubs the back of his head. "Hm. I guess I should have known." Garitol swings at Vander, hitting him in the gut. Vander folds over nicely, coughing and holding onto Garitol.

"Good, he's still standing. I guess you can. Anyone who can take that can date my daughter. Now finish cleaning. You get to go home early." Garitol walks back to the shop but goes upstairs and into his house.

Sounding extremely out of breath, he holds up his thumb. "You got it, boss." Still bending over with his hands on his knees, he says, "You're still coming over tonight, right?"

Emily staggers back, "Uh-huh."

Nick, with eyes wide open, says, "Damn, dude, you still alive?"

Coughing, Vander takes a step forward. "Just tell me, did you pass your test?"

Nick takes up an arm and helps him over to his workbench. "Magic is a funny thing. As long as you live, you pass the test."

Vander takes a deep breath. "All right, I'm calling in sick tonight. You guys do what you need. I'm going to finish up here and go pass out." Vander sends them off. Nick is done for the day, and so is Emily. They both go to the saloon to wait for him. Vander finishes up in a few hours with making himself a new weapon and cleaning up the shop.

After seeing her loving father hit someone like that for the first time, she is in shock and decides to wait for Vander to get in. She and Nick orders food and a bottle of wine and shares their day. Nick tells about the trial, and Emily says her day is bland. Emily becomes so distracted that she forgets to check on Rachel. Vander shows up with a beautiful sword. The back is all straight leading to the tip. The blade juts down a few inches and then smoothly transitions into the handguard, only beveling out slightly. Emily and Nick are wowed by it and the handiwork.

"This is like elven work, man. This is great. You should sell some of your good stuff and make a fortune. We could retire here real early," Nick says, holding it up and looking to see how straight the blade was.

"Well, I can't. The good stuff is for our adventure," Vander boasts and then breathes in through his teeth, putting an ice pack on his stomach.

"What adventure? We've been here for three months!"

"Yeah, where are you going?" Emily asked.

"I don't know, but humans came here from somewhere. I'm going to find out and see if I can't get back to home." Emily turns away, and Vander looks over. "What? I love it here, but I need to know what the hell is going on. *And* you're coming with me!"

Emily looks back. "What if I don't want to know or go anywhere? I have a family. This just shows that you care only for yourself."

Vander smiles back at her. "Hey, I want to take you along too, you know! I can't just leave you here. But I want to see this world before I die, and any step closer to the truth will make me happy. So come on, let's go."

Emily starts to nod her head. "We do need to leave, but soon, like tomorrow."

Vander replies, "We'll see. I have to make sure we have all we need."

After he is done eating, Vander hobbles up the stairs. Nick leans over. "You know he is faking it."

"I do." Emily giggles.

Nick smiles and leans back. "Must be love."

Emily follows and carries the sword, closing the door behind her.

Karach . . . karrrackkhu . . . Kaaccusa . . . Kaboom. Vander wakes up; he looks out the window, and fire is consuming the town. "What the devil?" He turns to Emily. She is still rubbing her eyes and wrapping herself in the blanket.

Two buildings are burning down not far from them. Emily yells, "Oh god, the orphanage!"

Vander rolls over the bed; he pulls out a bag. The room has armor and shields lining the walls. Vander pushes the bag to Emily. "Take our bags, and be ready. We may have to leave tonight."

Emily grabs it. "Hey, I thought you said you needed time to prep. What is this?"

Vander grabs his new sword and a spare and ties them to his belt. "I lied. I like this town too. I just had to prep myself to leave." A third building explodes. Vander pops out of the door at the same time Nick does.

Vander turns to him. "You see that?"

Nick, wide-eyed, says, "Shit yeah! Time to go."

"*No*! Time to see what is going on." Vander runs down the stairs, pulling down his shirt.

Outside, several buildings are up in flames. A girl in the middle of the street is faced with two crimson guards, both armed, one with an ax and the other a sword. A third lies on the ground, dead—burned to death and crispy. Vander and Nick jump out from the saloon and into the street. Just behind the girl, dust billows in the night sky. The soldier doesn't even move his eyes to them. "The crimson guards have been looking for you, and you know we won't quit unless you're dead!"

"Leave her alone!" Nick yells, putting his fists in the air.

"Hey, get ready to run, Nick. They may be more than we can take. But wait for Emily, she'll be right down." Vander takes a step in front of the girl.

The girl grabs his leg. "Emily is here?"

Vander gives a confused look. "Yes?"

The girl climbs up his leg. "I was looking for her!"

A crimson guard leaps into the air at them. Vander pulls a sword and blocks the ax from coming down on the girl's head. Nick moves his fingers into a weird shape, and flashes of light launches the guy across the road, taking out a stand. Other crimson guards start chopping down support beams to the second floor. The girl moves her hands too, setting three of the guards and the pillar on fire. A group of ten more guards approach. The girl stands up; and with a flick of her wrist, they fly into the air, with streams of fire streaking the sky. Three more buildings go up in flames.

Nick looks at her in astonishment. "We'll help you, just stop setting fires!"

The girl turns to him. "Deal."

Out of the saloon, an armor-covered woman appears. She drops a bag and clangs over to the middle of the road. She has so much metal on, so she can barely move. Vander thinks to himself, *Hey, that's my armor. I didn't ask her to bring all of it. And what is she doing, dropping that bag?*

Vander yells, "Emily, no!" Emily turns to see what he is looking at. Fred comes in from behind and stabs her through her chest. She only covered the front of herself with armor of the heaviest kind. The sword is holding up her chest plate; Fred was not able to go through. Blood gushes out from under the plate. She slinks to the ground and falls over, still moving her lips and reaching out to Vander.

Vander and Rachel both turn around as though in slow motion. "Noooo!" they yell at the top of their lungs.

Rachel pushes the boys to the side and lets out a war cry. A force around her ignites and propels Fred and the rest of his crimson guards miles away. At the same time, it obliterates three houses and crops for a tenth of a mile in that direction.

Rachel runs to Emily. She slides down to her knees and picks up her head. "Emily! Tell me you're all right. Please . . ." Rachel lifts off the helmet. Emily blinks rapidly and coughs up blood. Vander, still in shock, slowly walks to them.

Emily looks up to her. "Rachel, you're here. It's been so long."

Vander pulls her into his arms. Rachel reaches up and closes her eyes. Vander lets her down. He walks over and picks up his bag. "All right, Nick, are we ready to go?"

Nick looks over at him, tears welling in his eyes. He can't see his face. Thinking about how confusing this whole situation is, he answers, "Well, Vander, the people saw all of this, so let's go. None of them look happy at all." In fact, many people of the town are outside by now and have seen the death of one of their beloved townspeople. The bartender comes walking up out of the crowd. He has a bloodthirsty look in his eyes. He comes face-to-face with Vander.

Staring at the ground as though he could not lift his head, Vander says, "Sir, we're on our . . ."

The bartender hits him right in the jaw and knocks him to the ground. "You get out of here. It's not enough that every pillager, guard, and group that wants to pick on us can and will? We will not tolerate someone so destructive living among us. You were good, kid, but helping a dirty woman like that lead to deaths, that is irresponsible."

Vander staggers to his feet, holding his chin and giving him a deathly stare. "It was fun, but I won't be back."

The bartender rushes forward, leaning in with his fist in the air, and stops. Vander staggers back. "That was worse than any drunk," the bartender says.

How the Hell Do We Get Home From Here?

The bartender takes a step forward to Nick.
Nick says defensively, "All right, we're out."
Vander stands while Nick helps him. They grab what is lying there and start to walk out of town. Rachel runs to catch up.
Vander sneers at Rachel. "What do you want?"
Nick looks over to him. "Uh, we promised to help her."

Vander groans, and they continue to walk. As they leave, the crowd yells for the crimson guards to get them and all the obscenities one can imagine.

Chapter 7

An Excerpt from Joe's Manifesto

I actually love this land. Many think that I don't, and to them I say, "You know nothing." All I want is to be able to walk through the towns and be known, preferably without being asked to perform a miracle. You would have the same feelings if you were me. My favorite thing in life is to hear what good has been done in my name, J. Christman. As a god, of course, I would like to have everyone groveling at my feet; but eventually, looking at the back of heads gets dull.

People should be safe. I mean, goddamn it, is it that hard to love thy neighbor? Creating the crimson guard was the best thing I could have done. They monitor all my people and treat them the way I would like my people to be treated. The crimson guards are my representatives and spread my good name. Sometimes these people need to learn how to grow up.

I have lived for over five thousand years. Yes, wars have been started that people wanted me to end. I could have brought them to an end fast and safe. For the first few wars, I did, but as time went on, the same groups continued to fight. One problem that these people have *is* they don't understand what it's like to be God. To know all that is going on and have a discriminating eye, trying to let those beings make the right decision. I felt lower than low after the first death was caused because of social differences. If you read the manifesto, you'll know that I destroyed that village as an example that everyone dies equally. So, everyone should live equally. I live for my people. I bring the rain and the sun; shouldn't they just be happy that they are not starving? This last time, I have taken up my throne; and for one hundred years, there has been peace. There have only been small attacks by people with small minds. With the small-minded attacks, I send my crimson guards there, but they cannot be everywhere at once. They are my eyes and ears. I need them as they need me.

There is only one thing that has disturbed me in my lifetime. I decided to be a good leader of anamen and atone for sins cast in my name, such as war crimes, death cults, multimarriage cults (which lead to incest), and other famous acts of atrocity. I thought I was only giving these people enough power to help themselves live a comfortable life, but as in all civilizations, someone has to ruin it all. I met a young lady; her name was Zoey. She had been picked up for stealing. She admitted to it, for the vendor she was working for was not paying her enough to eat and live. It was her first time. I bet not her last. Once a dirtbag, always a dirtbag. She went into a trance and stared at me. It was dark, and I went to lie down. She reached across the bars and touched me. I saw the future in her mind. Images bounced around my head of peaceful places before and after wars, some I have seen come true. Then she spoke, "You will have a long rule, but only seven more returns are left for you." She did list off a few other things that would happen, like me controlling magic and helping to make one of the best warriors of all time. None of them bothered me; some even made me feel better about myself and what I'm going to do.

I am going to have fun in my next seven. Why would I put in this prophecy? Because I will not end. I put it in here so that I will have people try and take me on. I want all the traitors to be out of my planet.

Edwards Brothers, Inc.
Thorofare, NJ USA
December 5, 2011